About the Haywired serie

'Fans of Philip Reeve's Mortal Engi
debut novel, *Haywired* – published
compelling tale of unearthed family
diabolical plans to turn the world inside out, its up to 11 year
old Ludwig to rescue the world before any of the ghoulish
machines hunt him down. With a plot that's full of twists and
turns on every page, it's not to be missed.' – *Lovereading.co.uk*
(Debut Book of the Month.)

'The reader is gripped throughout... intrigue and suspicion pour
from the pages thanks to rich characterisation… just what mes-
merising spin will Alex Keller take us on in (the) future?'
– Natalie Crawford *The Solitary Bee* blog

'Keller has a fantastic writing style which draws you right into
the story. The pace is phenomenally fast too and I was never
bored. It was exciting and full of suspense - it's certainly not one
of those books where you can guess the ending... Rating: 5/5.'
– *Mostly Reading YA - A Blog about Young Adult Fiction*

'*Haywired* is very different to the steampunk books I have read
so far. The publishers are calling it a steampunk fairytale, and
I cannot come up with a better phrase to describe it... The
fairytale feel to the story is there from the very first page and
at times it is as if the Brothers Grimm were alive and well. The
story is deliciously dark in places...' – *Book Zone 4 Boys*

'Intelligently written, with plenty of wry humour that adds to its
adult readability. *Haywired* is a fun fantasy adventure full of
family secrets, a circus, pirates, steampunk machinery, dark
twists and some excellent grimness. I look forward to the next
one.' – *Un:Bound*

RE:WIRED

By Alex Keller

To Ciara
Have a great time
with ReWired!

MOGZILLA

RE:WIRED

First published by Mogzilla in spring 2011
Second printing autumn 2011

Paperback edition:
ISBN: 978-1-906132-34-7

Printed in the UK

http://www.mogzilla.co.uk/rewired

http://alexkelleruk.tumblr.com/

Recap

It's been months since Ludwig confronted his father in the Superbus' palace and he still can't believe what happened.

Almost a year before, he was living happily with his father, Mandrake; making strange contraptions in their castle. Then the HELOT had been designed, a machine that acted like the perfect slave, and Ludwig's life collapsed.

His father went crazy with the power the HELOTS could bring and started to build a HELOT army.

But that wasn't all. Ludwig overheard his father mention a brother he never knew existed, and their housekeeper accidentally let slip that his brother was still alive and being kept hidden in the castle by his father! Mandrake von Guggenstein had been lying to Ludwig for years.

Ludwig found his brother Hephaestus, a poor deformed giant, in the castle's cellars and brought him out from the darkness. Knowing they could no longer stay with their father, the two managed to escape.

Furious, Mandrake chased the brothers for months with his new HELOT army.

Sick of running, Ludwig eventually turned the tables and brought his father to justice.

Now, as Mandrake von Guggenstein waits for the day of his execution, in a faraway villa another prisoner awaits his fate...

Prologue

Gressin Theodos stood in one of the servants rooms in the east wing of the villa of his employer. His mouth was dry and he had to hold his hands to stop them shaking. The mission hadn't gone well.

He had been away for months, desperate to find Mandrake von Guggenstein, but he'd had no luck. He'd despaired. His employer didn't like failure.

Before he'd returned home, he guessed what his employer would do when she found out; so he'd devised a plan.

As soon as he was back, he sneaked into his employer's home, went to her private chambers, and searched for the jewellery case of which he had heard many rumours. His employer was very wealthy and the jewels must be worth millions. Then he would go to his family, gather them together, and run as far away as possible.

But he had been caught.

Right now, his employer stood in front of Gressin. She didn't look happy. Around her stood her other servants in a large circle and Gressin stood in the middle. They had been called to watch as their employer liked to set examples.

'Did you find Mandrake?' said his employer. Her arms crossed and her nails drumming against her lacy, delicate sleeve.

'I couldn't m'lady!' cried Gressin, wide-eyed and pleading. 'It were chaos over there! I went to the village like yer said and on to the castle, but they were empty. So I went t' Beacon and Mandrake... well...'

'Didn't yer hear? He'd taken over the city! He had these machines that did what he told them to. People couldn't even walk the streets without bein' taken by those things by the end of it.'

'His HELOTs,' said his employer. She sounded annoyed.

'That's right! No one could get near him! Then he were captured.' Gressin looked around the room. The others had their heads bowed. No one would meet his eye.

'It weren't my fault, m'lady!'

'Gressin, I'm very unhappy,' said his employer.

'I'm sorry!'

His employer shook her head and looked at him sympathetically.

'So am I, Gressin. And I must ask, what is that in your hand?'

Gressin looked down at the jewellery case in his hand.

'You failed and you were going to steal from me, Gressin,' said his employer.

Suddenly that smell entered the room and Gressin felt his stomach rise. There was movement behind him and he could hear an awful grinding sound. Gressin felt his arms and legs turn to jelly. He dared not turn around but the fear in the eyes of those near him was enough to know what was coming.

'Please, m'lady, have mercy!' he grovelled.

'Gressin, my family knows mercy achieves nothing and we have standards to maintain. You cannot expect us to act differently just for you. If it makes you feel better, this is not personal.'

'Please!' cried Gressin. 'I've worked fer your family fer years! No one is more loyal! I beg yer! I'm sorry about the jewels. I'll put 'em back and we can forget all about it, eh?'

'Why don't you have a look inside the jewellery case?' said his employer.

Gressin froze.

'No, please m'lady...'

'Open it.'

'No!'

'Sweetness,' said his employer, looking over Gressin's shoulder. 'Help him will you?'

Behind him, Gressin could hear her "Sweetness" move closer. The floor shuddered with every step. Panicking, Gressin jumped up, threw the jewellery case to the floor, and bolted for the nearest door; blind terror giving his legs strength. But he was still too slow. Something grabbed his waist and dragged him back.

'Yes, mother,' said the thing holding Gressin; its voice high, cruel and whining.

The jewellery case appeared before Gressin again. His employer's "Sweetness" held it and began opening it in front of him with one hand. Gressin screamed...

Chapter One:
Pashymore

Ludwig and The Captain stopped. The Captain was in his *new* new body, the one Hephaestus had only finished a week or so before. It was smaller than the old one. It let him move through the city without drawing attention to himself as long as he wore enough clothes. There were no skulls on it either. The Captain had been *very* specific about that.

In front of them was the old palace. It towered up into the sky, larger than all the other buildings around it by far. As its main entrance in Nikolis Square was busy with the day's event, they'd come to a smaller side door where two bored-looking guards stood watch. The guards waved them through.

'Has it started yet, sir?' asked one.

'Not yet,' said the Captain. 'But soon, mate. Very soon.'

Ludwig and the Captain made their way through the gloomy palace. Ludwig hadn't been inside since his father had been captured but it didn't look much different, although it was more crowded now with clerks running this way and that and guards standing to attention.

When they arrived in the audience chamber, Ludwig looked across the room and saw his grandmother standing alone near the balcony that looked out over the city. As he walked towards her, the others in the room caught sight of him. They went silent and stared. Soon they started to whisper to one another.

'Is that?'

'I think so...'

Ludwig ignored them as he walked towards his

grandmother. She was wearing a long black dress and sipped a glass of red wine slowly. She looked extremely angry.

'Ludwig, you're here at last,' she said when he came into view.

'I didn't have much choice,' Ludwig replied.

'–It's definitely him!' whispered someone nearby. 'Look he's with his grandmother–' All eyes were on Ludwig and his severe looking grandmother.

'Wait one moment, my dear,' said Matilda. She stepped forward and looked around at the other guests. 'Ladies and gentlemen, you are most rude! The boy and I have been through too much! Your stares and your sly words do not help one bit!'

Those watching looked at each other in a slightly embarrassed way and there was a small shuffling of feet, but their eyes remained fixed on Ludwig.

'*STOP STARING!*' A voice bellowed across the room making Ludwig jump. 'We may not have a prison any more but I'm sure we can come up with something appropriate if you don't find something a blasted sight more interesting than the boy, *RIGHT NOW!*'

Those nearby nearly dropped their glasses in shock before turning to one another. They were now making a pointed effort not to look in Ludwig's direction and spoke to each other even more loudly than before.

Ludwig looked to see who had called out. A man was now walking up to his grandmother. He was short, plump, and well-dressed; although his clothes were heavily creased and he looked very tired. A neat moustache sat above slightly over-large lips and below a small nose that was now wrinkled in disgust.

'I apologise, Matilda. Their manners are too poor.' He looked at Ludwig. 'So this is our saviour is it?'

'Harold, this is Ludwig von Guggenstein, my grandson.

Ludwig, this is Harold Pashymore, the only councillor left alive in Pallenway.'

'Hi,' said Ludwig.

'We owe you a great debt, my boy.' Councillor Pashymore pulled out a watch from his waistcoat, quickly looked at it then tucked it away again.

'Anyhow, come on,' he sighed. 'It's time this was put to bed.'

Ludwig walked with the Councillor and his grandmother over to a part of the large balcony that took up one side of the room, letting all those in the audience chamber look outside. Beyond was Nikolis Square and Pashymore looked out. Ludwig followed his gaze. Below, the square was full of people packed behind low fences, hanging out of windows and perched on rooftops. They were all here for one thing: to witness the death of Mandrake von Guggenstein.

'When this is done,' said Councillor Pashymore. 'We can move on with our lives.'

'I hope so,' said Ludwig quietly.

Chapter Two:
Kamaria Pili

In a corner of Beacon docks, out of the way of the cranes and dockworkers that lingered around the bigger piers, Hephaestus von Guggenstein was hard at work.

He stood inside one of the giant shed-like dry docks that lined the harbour here and there. He was covered in a long cloak he wore all the time these days, its hood thrown up to cover his face. Those with whom he worked knew he was different, but with the cloak on and hood up they forgot.

In front of him was a huge ship; a mass of wood and metal with three high masts, a smoke stack standing proudly on its deck, and on each side two great, round paddles. At this very moment, the ship was sliding into the sea for the very first time. Long, thick ropes stretched to teams of men who used all their might to hold the ship at bay like some colossal beast. In one of these teams stood Hephaestus.

'Easy!' he roared, grasping the rope in his hand tightly as the ship tried to pull away from him.

Behind, the men his grandmother had hired to help could only grunt in reply as they held onto the ropes, letting the ship slowly slide down a ramp into the waters.

'EASY!' Hephaestus cried again, straining on the coarse rope.

When the ship hit the water waves fled from it, breaking against the harbour wall. Hephaestus' men breathed a sigh a relief and rubbed their sore hands.

'We're there!' cried Hephaestus. 'Let her come about!'

The men grumbled but pulled at the ropes once again and

the ship turned in the water. Hephaestus watched as the ship soon lay resting against the dock and the workmen ran to tie it up.

Along its side read: *Kamaria Pili.*

'We're done,' said Hephaestus. He turned and called for his helpers to leave. They didn't have to be told twice. All of them were keen to get to the execution.

'You not comin', sir?' asked one.

Hephaestus shook his head from the depths of his hood. 'No,' he rumbled.

'Right you are,' said the workman, running to catch up with the others. Hephaestus was left alone. Or so he thought.

'You built that?' came a small voice behind him.

Hephaestus turned around to find a small boy staring up at the ship. He peered at the boy curiously.

'Yes,' he replied.

'Oh. That's clever, that is. I've been watching,' The boy regarded Hephaestus. 'Big, ain't yer?'

Hephaestus grunted. 'I suppose.'

'My mum says I should stay away from yer.' The boy screwed up his face. 'My mum says yer cursed. That's why yer so big an' ugly lookin'.'

Hephaestus turned and bent down so the boy could see into his hood. 'What do you think?' Hephaestus asked.

'I dunno. You *are* ugly lookin'. But so's Mrs Pollyherd and no one says she's cursed. D'you think yer are?'

Hephaestus smiled and stood up again. 'Maybe.'

'Don't you know?'

Hephaestus shrugged. 'No. No one's told me.'

The boy looked disappointed. 'Oh.'

Hephaestus looked around. 'Where are your friends?'

'In the square, 'course,' replied the boy. 'They don't want to miss what going to 'appen to *him.*'

Him, thought Hephaestus. They don't even need to say his

name any more. Now they use it to scare naughty children: be good or Mandrake will get you. And they weren't even Mandrake's HELOTs, not really...

'Aren't you goin'?' asked the boy.

'No,' growled Hephaestus.

The boy looked puzzled. 'Didn't yer lose someone?'

'In a way.'

'Don't yer want t' see 'im punished then? You got to punish someone when they've bin bad. I lost my dad, you see. He were in prison for thievin'. We... we never saw 'im again once those what-ya-ma-call-its turned up.'

'HELOTs. The machines. They were called HELOTs.'

'Oh, yeah. That's them. 'ELOTs.'

Hephaestus remembered the rows of HELOTS and the stacks of cubes that held the minds of the inmates of Beacon prison. You took a mind, you put it in cube, you put the cube in a HELOT and it would do what you commanded. A perfect slave.

'I'm sorry,' said Hephaestus.

'Ain't your fault,' said the boy. 'Besides, didn't know 'im much. Mum always said he'd come to a bad end anyway.'

'Don't you want to go?'

The boy shuffled his feet and stared at the ground. 'I saw a dead man in the street once when the 'ELOTs were 'ere. I don't want to see another.'

Hephaestus stared at the boy at a loss as to what to say. Instead, his hand went to the tool-belt around his waist. He took a wrench and held it out.

'Would you like to help me instead?'

The boy looked at the wrench and then at Hephaestus. 'You sure you ain't cursed?' he asked, trying to look into the darkness of Hephaestus' face again.

'Pretty sure.'

The boy grinned. 'Well... all right then.'

Chapter Three:
Execution of the Past

In the square below, Ludwig watched as the doors were thrown open by the palace guard. Towards the front of the square, people were clambering to get the best view and crushing those around them while the guards pushed them back. Then the crowd fell silent and stared. Out from behind the doors came two rows of guards, rifles in hand, masks covering their faces. They marched to the edges of the human corridor that led from the palace to the gallows, stopped, turned, and stood looking into the people of Beacon. Behind the guards came an ugly tractor. It trudged along on caterpillar treads, pouring foul, black smoke into the air. It was driven by a hooded man and on its back was a cage. In the cage was Ludwig's father.

Ludwig realised he was holding his breath.

Mandrake sat on a stool in the middle of the cage with his long dark hair hanging down in knots, hiding his face from the crowd. He looked even thinner than Ludwig remembered if that was possible.

The tractor moved on towards the gallows where Ludwig could just about make out a noose swinging in the light breeze. It sent a shiver down his spine and Ludwig bit his tongue. Suddenly he wanted to shout out; to do something that would delay this terrible event; but he knew this had to be done and done publicly, so all would know the man of their nightmares was dead and they could live again.

The tractor stopped and the hooded driver reached down and pulled a lever. A clawed arm unfolded itself from the tractor's rear that extended, hooked on to Mandrake's cage, and hauled it up onto the platform. Ludwig recognised the mechanism. He had built it with his father five years ago. He had been told it was to help dockworkers unload the ships. Perhaps it had even been used in such a way once.

After Mandrake had been set down, the hooded man stepped off the tractor and walked up the steps to take his place. Then he waited and the crowd fell silent.

There was a buzz of static that echoed around the square, followed by councillor Pashymore's voice.

'Citizens of Beacon,' said the councillor. 'You are all here to witness the execution of Mandrake von Guggenstein, traitor and murderer.'

Ludwig saw councillor Pashymore had an ampliphone in his hands that let his voice travel in such a manner. He listened on as the crowd opened up with a bloody, deafening cheer.

'Mandrake von Guggenstein,' he continued, 'The charges against you are thus: you conspired to overthrow the government and take Pallenway and its capital, Beacon, for yourself. Through doing so, you were responsible for the deaths of a great many people. I am told a list of those recorded as perishing due to your actions or through the actions of your HELOTs has been read to you every day of your incarceration, and I am satisfied you are fully aware of your crimes. Do you have anything to say before the judgement is carried out?'

The hooded man next to Mandrake's cage had another ampliphone in his hand. He placed it on the ground next to his prisoner and Mandrake reached down, took the ampliphone, and lifted it to his mouth.

'No. I do not.'

Ludwig looked across the square and saw the crowd was annoyed. They expected more. Mad ravings; cackling laughter; anything. This was the man of their nightmares after all. To just say "no" wasn't right.

'So be it–' began the councillor.

'Wait,' said Mandrake, holding up a hand.

Ah, thought the crowd. Here it comes…

'I wish to apologise to my sons. Ludwig, Hephaestus, I hope you can hear this. I am so very sorry; truly I am. I hope some day you may find it in your hearts to forgive me. Please, live well without me. That is all.'

Ludwig felt his throat tighten and he jumped when Pashymore put a hand on his shoulder. Even the crowd looked uncomfortable.

'I- I will make sure they hear,' replied Pashymore. He turned, lent down, and moved the ampliphone away from his mouth. 'Ludwig, are you ready?' he whispered before glancing at Matilda.

Ludwig nodded but didn't say a word.

Pashymore lifted the ampliphone back to his mouth.

'Executioner, do your duty.'

The hooded man looked up at the balcony, saluted, then took an iron key from his coat and went over to the door of Mandrake's cage. He unlocked it and Mandrake stepped out. The executioner heard the crowd drawing breath but to his surprise, when he turned back around, they were no longer looking at him or Mandrake. He followed their gaze to the other side of the square.

At the far end of the square was something truly awful. A great mechanical skeleton stood over the crowd so big it nearly filled the main entrance to the square. It was perhaps twenty feet tall and hissed and spluttered. It started to move and as it got closer, the executioner could see a pale figure on its front tied to the machine with metal bands. It was at this point the executioner started to whimper.

The crowd fell back, too shocked to even scream at first. Ludwig watched in horror as the machine strode through them, not caring where its feet came down. As it got closer, he could see the machine more clearly. The figure strapped to its chest appeared to be dead if that was even possible. Ludwig spied wires pouring out from the corpse and into the machine. Occasionally the body would jerk as if shocked, throwing its head from one side to another; but otherwise its limbs and head hung loosely, simply swaying with each step like some kind of gruesome decoration.

As it made its way towards the scaffolding the crowd found their voices. Their screams were louder than their earlier cheers.

Ludwig turned. There was a commotion behind him. In the viewing chamber, the guests were either fleeing or simply staring, dumbstruck with terror. Then he saw the Captain and his old friend Sir Notsworth running towards him.

'Ludwig! We must go!' shouted Sir Notsworth.

'No... wait,' said Ludwig. For some reason he wasn't scared. He looked back and saw the machine moved with purpose; it was only here for one thing. Ludwig watched as the machine knocked the executioner aside, reached out, and grabbed his father before striding out of the square at great speed, leaving a trail of badly hurt people in its wake. The only words Ludwig heard over the screaming were from his father, whose voice had echoed over the square through the ampliphone.

'Grilsgarter?'

Chapter Four:
Getaway

Hephaestus was standing on the deck of the *Kamaria Pili* when he heard cries coming from the far end of the dock.

'What's going on?' asked the boy Hephaestus had met earlier, his head popping up from one of the hatches that led below.

'Wait here,' said Hephaestus. 'This doesn't sound good.'

Hephaestus ran down the *Kamaria's* gangplank and along the wharf towards the point where Thelick Street met the docks. When he got closer, he saw people pouring out of the street in a panic. Some even jumped into the sea without pausing while others were simply pushed into the water by those behind, desperate to get away. Moments later, a great machine stormed out the street and onto the docks, knocking down anyone nearby. In one of its claws, Hephaestus saw a person. He looked closer.

Oh no!

Nearby was a ship, its engines running. Hephaestus watched as the machine jumped off the dock and onto the ship's deck. The ship's engines roared as the machine landed and Hephaestus heard a loud thud when its feet touched down. The ship then made its way out to sea while Hephaestus looked on, helpless; he could do nothing but watch as the evil-looking machine looked back at the chaos it had caused.

'What happened?' asked the boy, appearing at Hephaestus' side.

'Something terrible,' replied Hephaestus. 'I have to go home.'

'Has your father *ever* mentioned someone called "Grilsgarter"?' Councillor Pashymore shouted at Ludwig. They were back at Matilda's house now and the Councillor's earlier kindness had now gone. Now he was an inferno of rage and anger.

After his father had been taken, Ludwig had been carried all the way home by Sir Notsworth, who wouldn't let anyone else touch him, even the Captain. Unfortunately Sir Notsworth had forgotten Ludwig was getting older, and between Ludwig's struggling and his size, this had been too much for the explorer, who was now sitting wheezing and spluttering in a corner while the councillor interrogated Ludwig.

Councillor Pashymore grabbed Ludwig by the shoulders and shook him. 'Listen to me, boy! Has he ever said anything?'

'No! Never!' cried Ludwig. 'Let go of me!'

'Leave him alone! You'll hurt him!' cried Ludwig's grandmother.

'Are you sure?' asked Pashymore, still holding Ludwig tight. 'I don't suppose your father got bored one day and decided to make that thing for fun? Azmon knows what other nightmares have been thought up in that twisted head of his!'

'No! I told you!' shouted Ludwig, pulling away. Pashymore went to grab him again but he slipped through the councillor's fingers.

Councillor Pashymore turned to the others.

'None of you?' he bellowed. 'None of you have heard of this "Grilsgarter"? Not one? I find this hard to believe. Matilda. I thought you had been watching him for years!'

'Mandrake moved around a lot before he went back to Little Wainesford,' she replied as calmly as she could. 'He could have met all sorts of people on his travels. What about you? He worked for your government before the HELOT attack. You kept that quiet enough.'

'That was nothing to do with me,' said the Councillor sharply. He paced around. 'Matilda, that... thing was a corpse! Has he got an army of them too? Should we just lay down and wait for the worst?'

'I have no idea who or what it was, Councillor. Nor do you. Don't jump to conclusions. However, I do know that if he had an army of them then why would only one turn up? It doesn't make sense.'

Pashymore slumped onto a chair next to Sir Notsworth whose cheeks were finally starting to lose their redness. The Councillor held his head in his hands. 'Your blasted son is loose again, Matilda. Beacon has barely recovered from his last attack.'

'We will get him back,' she replied.

'You'd better!'

The front door swung open and Hephaestus stepped in. 'I saw father!' he called out frantically but he stopped when he saw the other's faces. 'I guess you know...'

'What did you see, mate?' asked the Captain.

'Not much. Some kind of machine ran to the docks and onto a ship. It sailed away before I could do anything.'

Pashymore looked up. 'He's left the city?' he groaned. 'We've got no chance of finding him now.'

'Not so fast, mate,' said the Captain. 'Hephaestus, did you notice anything about the ship? A flag maybe, or a name?'

Hephaestus shook his head. 'No.'

'Maybe he won't come back,' said Ludwig. 'Maybe he just didn't want to die.'

'I'm not counting on it,' said Pashymore, 'and that's not his decision to make. No, I need your father on the end of that noose and so does the city. I'm sorry to be harsh, boy, but that's the long and short of it.'

'We'll ignore your unfortunate turn of phrase,' said Matilda, coldly. 'As we know you are under a lot of pressure.'

'Pressure, Matilda? That's barely the half of it! Your son murdered all the other Councillors! I'm the only one left! Can you imagine what that's like? What should I do? You tell me. I've half a mind to resign and go and live out the rest of my life in a cave half way up a mountain. Beacon will be a wasteland before long, your son will see to that.'

'We don't know what's going on,' Matilda replied. 'But we do need to get him back. If that machine is another type of HELOT we haven't seen before then we are all in very serious danger.'

'I don't care,' said Councillor Pashymore. 'I'm going to put a bounty on your son's head. 'I'll put a price on him so high that every hunter from here to hell will be after him. '

'If you must, Pashymore,' said Matilda quietly.

Then she called for her butler to prepare the coaches. 'Where are we goin'?' asked the Captain.

'Little Wainesford,' Matilda replied. 'If this Grilsgarter is someone from Mandrake's past, a clue to his whereabouts may be there. We have little else to go on. If we don't learn anything at the castle, I can speak to some people on the continent, but it could take months to hear back. This is the best way.'

'We could try—' began the Captain.

'No,' said Matilda. 'Not him.'

The Captain nodded. 'As you say.'

'We will leave at first light tomorrow.'

'Do what you like, Matilda,' said Councillor Pashymore. 'But I want him back, dead or alive and as soon as possible. Remember: if you don't get him, someone else will.'

He got up and walked out of the mansion, saying nothing more.

Chapter Five: Homecoming

The next day, Ludwig felt nervous as his grandmother's carriage trundled towards his old home. He hadn't been back to Little Wainesford since he ran away with Hephaestus all those months ago, but he remembered Mr Shawlworth's story well; the old gardener had sat down in his grandmother's dining room and told everyone of the grim things that had happened after Ludwig and Hephaestus left. How all the villagers had been taken and then put into his father's machines. Ludwig felt sick at the memory. They were people Ludwig had lived with all his life.

Ludwig was also surprised his grandmother wanted him to come along. He expected to be told to stay at home but instead she had almost pushed him into a carriage. 'You're not leaving my sight,' was all she said as an explanation.

Soon enough Little Wainesford came into view after an uneventful journey. Ludwig leaned out of the carriage and saw the houses and few shops that made up the village huddled together in the middle of familiar fields. The church spire poked out from the low roofs and beyond were the trees that hid Castle Guggenstein.

At the edge of the village the carriage came to a halt. When Ludwig stepped out on to the dusty road he heard a familiar voice.

'Greetin's!'

Ludwig looked around and saw Mr Shawlworth, his father's old gardener, coming out of one of the nearby cottages. Mr Shawlworth had been there when Hephaestus and the Captain blew up Beacon prison. During that time, Mr Shawlworth had been injured by Jack, a cruel man Ludwig's father had turned into a HELOT that looked like some monstrous metal spider. After Ludwig's father had been captured, Mr Shawlworth had gone back to Little Wainesford after he had recovered from his wound. With Mr Shawlworth was a young, sad-looking couple carrying some small things to a waiting cart.

'What're you lot doin' 'ere?' the old gardener asked when he got closer. Ludwig noticed he was still walking with a limp and had a cane in one hand.

'Arthur Shawlworth, it's good to see you!' replied Matilda, stepping out of the carriage behind Ludwig. She walked over, leaned forward and pecked him on each cheek.

'And you Matilda, as always.' Mr Shawlworth went up to each person in turn and shook their hands. When he got to Ludwig, he gave him a pat on the head. 'Hello lad. How have you been doing? City life's a bit different from here, eh?'

Ludwig nodded. 'Yes, Mr Shawlworth.'

'How have you been?' asked Matilda.

'Well enough I suppose,' replied Mr Shawlworth. 'I've been tryin' to sort the place out after you-know-what happened.' He looked over to the couple he had been with. They were going back into the cottage. 'People who had family in Little Wainesford have been coming for their relatives' things.' Ludwig looked over to the other nearby cottages and spotted more people taking things out and loading them onto carts. When they had finished, they left in such a hurry they barely gave a goodbye to Mr Shawlworth as they shot past and away.

'No one'll stay long and the village will just be a ruin soon,' explained Mr Shawlworth. He shook his head sadly and looked at the others. 'Anyway, that's by the by. Life goes on. What're you lot doin' here?'

Matilda explained why they had come to Little Wainesford and Mr Shawlworth was horrified.

'Mandrake escaped!' Oh, say it ain't so! After all that's happened!'

'I don't expect he'll come back here,' replied Matilda. 'But perhaps you should get everyone to leave as soon as they've finished their business just in case.'

'I will, Matilda, I will. Let's get you to the castle as quickly as possible so we can all get out of here. Come on.' The old gardener turned and started hobbling away at quite a pace. The rest followed.

As they walked through Little Wainesford, Ludwig looked around. There was *The Lantern and Parapet* where Ludwig had heard singing and laughter whenever he had gone with his father on their evening strolls. Across the road was the church with its old graveyard where the blue flowers grew. And there was the blacksmiths and there was the little shop that sold boiled sweets, and over the fields Ludwig spied the mill with its great wheel still turning ponderously on the river. It was all familiar but now very different. Ludwig felt sad to think of everything that had been lost.

At the end of the village was the short path that led to Ludwig's old home. They trekked on and Castle Guggenstein appeared before them, its low towers poking out between the trees. It was just as Ludwig remembered it. The dark stone walls looked as solid as ever.

'Wait here,' said the Captain.

Everyone stopped and watched the Captain make his way up the dirt path that opened up in front the castle's gates. The gates themselves hung ajar, creaking in the wind and barely attached to their hinges. Before, they could only be opened in a particular way, a means devised by Ludwig's father to keep out unwanted guests; now anyone could wander in. Ludwig watched the Captain walk through the gate and then into the courtyard, and finally into the castle itself. After a few minutes, he appeared again at the main door.

'It looks safe,' he called out.

When they got to the Captain, he pushed open the main door further and they stepped through. Inside, Ludwig was shocked to find all his father's things had gone. He poked his head into the kitchen then the long gallery and finally the music room. They were all bare. Finally, he ran up to the staircase and through the corridors and stairwells to his old room. He pushed the door open and found it was as empty as all the rest. The bed, the drawers, everything had gone.

'What happened?' he asked Mr Shawlworth when he got back to the main hall.

'Looters. When your father was caught they knew it was safe to come and take what they wanted. They took anything that wasn't nailed down. Bits and pieces have gone from the village too. They even pillaged my shed, the blighters.'

'That's terrible.'

'Jus' people bein' people. Probably thought somethin' was owed after what your father did.'

'Maybe...'

'Come on, lad,' said Mr Shawlworth. 'We've got work to do.'

'Begin searching the castle,' said Matilda. 'Don't leave a stone unturned. We must find out who this "Grilsgarter" is at all costs.' She stopped and looked around. 'Ludwig my dear, please come with me.'

'Off you go,' said Mr Shawlworth gently as he went off into the garden to see if any plants could be saved.

Ludwig followed his grandmother up the broad staircase that led to the first floor landing. At the top, he saw the library doors were open and he quickly peeked through. In the library the shelves had been pulled down and all the books were gone except for a few lonely, torn pages scattered on the floor. It was a miserable sight.

'They even took our books,' muttered Ludwig.

'This way, dear,' said his grandmother, gently pressing on his shoulder. 'Don't worry, we can get more.'

Ludwig followed his grandmother past the library and towards his father's private rooms.

'So you lived all the way down here?' asked Mr Shawlworth as he and Hephaestus descended into the darkness of the cellars.

'Yes,' said Hephaestus.

'I can't imagine what that was like.'

When they got to the bottom of the stairwell, Sir Notworth's lantern-light caught on the rows and rows of wine bottles that lined the first room in the cellars. 'Ah...' he said, a broad smile spreading across his face. He ran to the racks and pulled out the first bottle he came to, blowing off the dust. 'Well, well, well! This is a '78 Uppswell Reserve! I don't suppose...'

'They'll only be taken once anyone has the nerve to come down here,' said Hephaestus. 'Might as well be you.'

Hephaestus left Sir Notsworth and made his way deeper into the cellar. Eventually he came to the door to his chambers. He opened it and stepped through.

'I think what we are looking for will be in here,' said Matilda, looking at the door to Mandrake's rooms. She pushed open a door and led Ludwig inside.

His father's rooms were just as torn and ransacked as the rest of the castle. Ludwig had rarely entered this place even when he had lived here. It felt strange even now; as if he were trespassing. He could still remember his father's face when he had been caught wandering about here when he was younger. Mandrake fumed at Ludwig and had sent him to bed without dinner that night. Ludwig felt his father's disapproving eyes were still on him.

However, one thing caught Ludwig's eye. At the end of one small corridor that ran between the bedroom and the bathroom was a closed door. Across its surface were a few scratches and scrapes, it looked like people had tried to break it down but had failed.

His study, thought Ludwig.

'Your grandfather made that door so only he could get inside,' explained Matilda. 'Your father knew the secret too but I had never thought to ask. I don't suppose...'

Ludwig shook his head. 'No, father didn't tell me either.'

Ludwig walked up to the door and looked at it carefully. It was completely smooth; no keyhole or door-handle could be found. He ran his fingers over it slowly and found it was cold and smooth to touch, Ludwig could only guess at what it was made from. He drummed his fingers on the door and noticed he could hear a faint sound, like bells chiming.

Hephaestus sat on his bed and looked around. This place had been his home from before he could remember until nearly a year ago. He knew every chipped stone and every crack in the ceiling. He also knew every one of the paintings that covered the walls as he had done each one himself. He realised he felt sad. He missed this room. It may have been little bigger than a prison cell, but it had been his to do with as he pleased.

In one corner was a box full old knick-knacks he had no use for. He emptied the box on the floor then placed it on the bed. He looked around. On the desk opposite his bed were a few books. He picked them up and dropped them in the box. Then he turned to the paintings. He reached up, took the first and rolled it up carefully. On his desk was a candle. He lit it and poured a tiny amount of wax on the rolled up painting to hold it in place before placing it into the box.

'Do you have any idea how to get in?' asked Matilda. 'If there is anything that could help us I am sure it will be behind that door. I would ask the Captain to break it down but I fear even he would fail at that.'

'No,' replied Ludwig, 'but I know someone who might.' Ludwig ran back to the landing above the main hall. 'Notsworth? Are you there?' he called down.

'Hullo,' Notsworth called back, appearing below. He was covered in dust with a bottle of wine in one hand and a lantern in the other. Ludwig guessed he must have been in the cellar. If he had found the wine it meant even the looters weren't brave enough to venture down there. Ludwig didn't blame them.

'You've been in father's study before haven't you? I remember the last time you visited.'

'Only that once, lad,' Sir Notsworth called back. 'Why?'

'Did father use a key to get in?'

'Funny you should say that. No, he just stopped and tapped on the door. I thought it was odd at the time.'

'Thank you, Notsworth!' Ludwig ran to his grandmother. 'I think I know what to do,' he said. He rested his head on the study door and began tapping.

Tap, tap, tap-tap-tap...

There was a click and the door swung open.

'What did you do?' asked his grandmother, completely

surprised.

'It's a piano,' explained Ludwig. 'You play a melody on it and it opens.'

Matilda laughed sadly. 'So like your grandfather. He hated violence. Try to break the door down and you'll never get in, but play it a song... How did you know what to play?'

'I didn't. I just played the first thing that came into my head. I don't think it matters.'

'Your grandfather was a very strange man but a very good one,' said Matilda. 'I wish you could have met him. You and he are so alike.' She pushed open the study door. 'Come, there's no time to waste. I imagine Pashymore is having his bounty posters printed as we speak.'

They walked through into Mandrake's study. It was as cluttered and full as it must have been when Ludwig's father first left with the HELOTs to attack Beacon. To one side were a couple of chairs, a small table with a glass and a bottle on it, and a broad, ornate fireplace was set into the wall. The whole room was neat and spoke of a very ordered mind.

'You try his desk,' said Matilda. 'I'll start over here.'

Matilda went to the far corner of the room where some tall cabinets lent against a wall. Ludwig went over to his father's desk. He picked up one paper after another, read each in turn, then put it down again when he saw it wasn't what he wanted.

As he continued his search, he noticed a small, ordinary-looking box on the desk. It wasn't big enough to hold any letters but it somehow looked out of place amongst the clutter. Ludwig reached out and opened it. To his surprise, inside he found a small model of a HELOT. It must have been only a couple of inches high but it was exact in every way. He reached in and went to pick it up...

'Ah!' he cried out in surprise. The little HELOT had leapt out of his reach!

Ludwig watched, shocked, as the tiny machine scuttled across the desk and jumped off onto the ground.

It's working! Ludwig thought. But how...? The cubes his father had used to store the minds of those he killed to make the HELOTs work were bigger than the whole of this little one. It was impossible.

Ludwig dived after the machine but the little HELOT was fast. It ran under the desk and stayed there while Ludwig rolled around on the ground.

'What are you doing?' called his grandmother from the other side of the room. 'We've no time to waste. Have you found something?'

'No! Nothing!' Ludwig called back. 'I just dropped something, that's all!'

Ludwig looked at his grandmother but she was engrossed in some papers in her hand, and didn't seem to have noticed the little HELOT. For some reason he thought it wouldn't be a good idea to tell his grandmother of what he found; she would only disapprove. Once he was sure his grandmother wasn't coming to investigate, Ludwig slowly pulled the desk back and found the HELOT cowering in a corner.

'Don't worry,' he whispered, stepping closer.

When he was close enough, he reached out and caught the thing in his hands, pressing his palms together so its arms were pinned down. The machine's mechanisms whined as it tried to get free.

'Shhh,' said Ludwig quietly. 'It's okay.'

He waited and the machine slowly stopped struggling. He opened his hands and found the little HELOT was shaking but not trying to run away.

Ludwig looked at it puzzled. What are you? He wondered.

'Ludwig? What have you got there?' called his Grandmother. 'You've found something, haven't you?'

'Not yet!' Ludwig called back. He slipped the machine into his pocket, buttoned it up, and then went back to searching the desk again. He could feel the HELOT scrabbling about but he would wait until he was alone before he examined it further.

Still shocked by his find, Ludwig carried on looking through the papers on his father's desk for a few more minutes but he had no luck finding anything that would tell them who this Grilsgarter was. All he found were old designs or the notes to go with them, some of which Ludwig recognised, and that was it.

Leaving the top of the desk, he moved to the drawers and opened the first he came to. Within was a pile of unopened letters all addressed to his father. *Grilsgarter... Grilsgarter,* Ludwig thought to himself, opening each one in turn and checking the signature at the bottom.

Nothing... nothing... nothing...ah!

And there it was. The writing was awful; all jagged lines and the pen must have been pressed so hard it nearly tore the paper. Ludwig read:

MANDRAKE,

YOU HAVE NOT BEEN IN CONTACT FOR SOME TIME. REMEMBER WHAT YOU OWE. I WILL TAKE WHAT WAS PROMISED, BE SURE OF THAT. SEND WORD THROUGH THE PAINTED MAN. I EXPECT TO HEAR FROM YOU SOON. IF NOT, THERE WILL BE CONSEQUENCES.

- GRILSGARTER

'Grandmother!' Ludwig called out. He turned and saw his Grandmother reading from a folder. Her face was white as a sheet. 'Grandmother?' said Ludwig again. He walked up to her and touched her on the arm.

'Ludwig!' she cried out, startled. 'Oh, my dear, I'm sorry... What– what is it?' She ran her hands through Ludwig's hair frantically and Ludwig saw her eyes were wide. She was terribly worried.

'What were you reading?' Ludwig asked.

'Nothing,' said his grandmother. She quickly put the folder back where she found it and closed the cabinet door. 'It was just something about your grandfather. What have you got there, come now.'

Ludwig gave his grandmother the letter and she read it.

'Oh no...' she said in a hushed tone. She walked past Ludwig, out of the study, and back towards the main hall.

Ludwig followed and felt the HELOT scrabbling away in his pocket.'

Stop it!' he hissed and to his surprise the HELOT calmed down.

'Captain!' Matilda cried out when she got to the landing. She lent out and looked towards the great hall below. 'Captain? Where are you?'

'I'm here, m'lady,' said the Captain, coming up the stairs with Sir Notsworth, Hephaestus, and Mr Shawlworth behind him. When they got to the landing, Matilda passed the Captain the note and he read it.

'So we do have to see him,' said the Captain once he had finished.

'I don't like it but it appears we've no choice. If he can tell us where Mandrake might be...'

'What are you talking about?' asked Ludwig. 'Who's the Painted Man?'

'An old acquaintance of mine,' said the Captain. He turned to Hephaestus who had appeared with a box full of things in his arms. Sir Notsworth was behind him with another box full of bottles of wine. 'Is the *Kamaria* ready?' the Captain asked.

'Just about,' replied Hephaestus. 'Why?'

'We've got a long journey ahead of us.'

'Where are we going?' asked Ludwig.

'I want to go with the Captain!' said Ludwig crossly. He sat in his grandmother's carriage as they began to make their way home. The others, seeing a fight was about to break out in the von Guggenstein household, crowded into the other carriage to stay out of the way, including Hephaestus. Ludwig's grandmother had forbidden Ludwig to go with the Captain and he wasn't happy.

'I should go,' said Ludwig.

'No, dear,' replied Matilda. 'The Painted Man is extremely dangerous and he lives a long way away. I understand why you want to help but you're not needed this time. Stay in Pallenway where it is safe and you will see everyone again soon enough.'

'But–' began Ludwig.

'No "buts",' said Matilda sharply. 'You're staying here and that's final.'

'I was the one who saved everyone last time. I can do it again.'

'No you can't, Ludwig. You were reckless to go after your father before but the HELOTs couldn't hurt you and your father wouldn't. We don't know what we are dealing with this time. After what happened in Nikolis Square, I doubt this Grilsgarter has any problem with killing even you. And the Painted Man...' she trailed off.

'Who is the Painted Man?' Ludwig asked.

'The Captain told you. He is someone from the Captain's past who I wouldn't like to meet again. I certainly don't want you to meet him either.'

'This isn't fair.'

'Stop it, Ludwig.'

Ludwig huffed, crossed his arms and looked out of the carriage window. He couldn't see the castle but to his surprise, he could see smoke rising from behind the trees where castle Guggenstein stood.

'Stop!'

'What's wrong, dear?' asked Matilda.

'The castle! It's on fire!'

'Ludwig...' began his grandmother.

Ludwig turned to her. 'There's smoke and everything!' He jumped up and banged on the roof. 'Stop!' he cried and the carriage came to a halt. He ran out. 'Quick! Get water!'

'Wait,' called his grandmother.

Ludwig turned. 'Come on! We have to–!' But then he saw the look on his grandmother's face. 'but, but–'

'Ludwig, listen, I am as upset about this as you are but trust me, it needed to be done.'

Ludwig's face fell. 'You did this?'

'Yes, dear.'

'No!' Ludwig dropped to the ground, like a marionette with its strings cut.

'The castle isn't your home any more,' said his grandmother. 'It's a stack of stones haunted by old memories and a terrible past. It's better to burn it down than to leave it standing. It does no one any good for it to remain.'

Ludwig was too shocked to reply. He got up again and slumped back into the carriage. He said nothing for the rest of the journey.

He could feel the HELOT squirming in his pocket all the way back to Beacon.

⚙

Chapter Six:
Little Revelation

It was dark by the time they returned to Beacon. When they got home, Ludwig darted from his grandmother's carriage and into the mansion. He ran upstairs in order to hide his tears from the others and jumped on his bed. No one else had stopped it, he thought. His home had just been burned down and no one cared. Sir Notsworth just stared at his shuffling feet; Mr Shawlworth just watched in that quiet way of his; and even Hephaestus didn't seem upset.

But Ludwig had saved one thing at least.

He got up again then took a chair and angled it under the door-handle so it couldn't be opened from the outside. Now, feeling safe, he got down onto the floor and undid his pocket.

The HELOT crawled out of his hand and onto the floor. Ludwig watched it as it scurried about clumsily. It seemed confused to where it was at first but then it bolted and tried to hide. Before it got very far Ludwig grabbed it again. He brought it up to his eyes and frowned.

'What are you?'

Suddenly there was a bang on his door. Despite knowing the door wouldn't open, Ludwig quickly stuffed the HELOT back into his pocket again.

'Hello?'

'Ludwig?' came Hephaestus' voice. 'Are you there?' The handle moved a few times, but the chair kept the door closed. 'Ludwig, please open the door.'

'Go away!' Ludwig called back.

'I want to speak to you.'

'And I want to be alone, please. I'll— I'll find you later.'

Ludwig heard his brother sigh. 'If you wish but I'm going to bed. It's been a long day. If I don't see you tonight we'll speak tomorrow, but for what it's worth I think grandmother was right to do what she did.'

Ludwig didn't reply.

'Night,' said Hephaestus through the door.

Once Ludwig heard his brother's footsteps fade he went over to the dresser. On it were a couple of plates of food that his grandmother's servants had left there as a snack if Ludwig felt hungry. He walked over to them, took a piece of cheese, and laid it on the floor. Then he took the HELOT and put it down. Sure enough, the HELOT walked over and started bashing it head against the cheese, trying to eat despite it having no mouth.

You're not human, thought Ludwig, feeling very relieved. *You're a mouse!*

While Ludwig examined the little HELOT and Hephaestus prepared for bed, Matilda sat in her drawing room. The Captain stood opposite her.

'Was that really necessary?' asked the Captain. 'It was their home after all.'

'Yes,' said Matilda.

'You're takin' away their past.'

Matilda looked at the Captain and he saw a fierceness in her eyes. The same fierceness he had seen when they had first met years ago.

'It was an awful past,' said Matilda. 'They'd do better to forget it ever happened.'

'Matilda —'

'Don't forget your position here, Captain,' she said quickly.

'You work for me. If I want your advice I'll ask for it.'

The Captain rocked back in his chair, shocked at what he had heard. She had never spoken to him like that before.

'Apologies, Mat– m'lady,' he said. He stood up and turned to leave. 'I know my place all right. I'll leave yer be.'

But before he could take another step, Matilda's hand was on his arm.

'Wait. Captain. I'm sorry. It's been a trying few days. I didn't mean that. You know I don't think of you as a servant. But with Mandrake out there, Ludwig being difficult, and Hephaestus wrapped up in his misery, everything seems to be coming apart.'

He looked at her again. The fierceness had gone, leaving a tired old woman.

'That place was full of monstrous things,' she continued. 'Not just memories. In Mandrake's study I read– no, I will not say, I cannot bear to believe it; but burning that place was for the best. The boys can start new lives'

'But still–'

'Please Captain, trust me. We are friends are we not?'

'Yes Matilda, we are.'

'Then trust me, I beg you. Mandrake is my son but his actions are so unforgivable I cannot bear to think of them.'

'I do trust you, yer know that. Good night.' The Captain then left for his own room, leaving Matilda in peace.

Upstairs, as the Captain readied himself for sleep, he couldn't help but wonder what Matilda was speaking about. What secrets had she found to make her burn down her family home? But it wasn't in the Captain's nature to pry. He had secrets enough of his own to worry about. Matilda would tell him in time if she thought she needed to.

There was a click and the light in the Captain's eyes died. He slept and dreamt of the sea.

Chapter Seven: Stowaway

The next morning, Ludwig sat at a table in the garden in the shade of a broad tree. A pencil was in his hand. He was trying hard to listen to Mr Yewsreddy but it was proving impossible. His tutor's voice droned into his ear like a buzzing insect Ludwig wished he could swat away. When his father had taught him Ludwig had listened fascinated to the explanations of all the strange and wonderful things in the world. Mr Yewsreddy, however, treated learning simply as a collection of bits of information that were to be remembered at all costs yet never used for anything other than exams, of which he was extremely keen and gave one almost every other day. Ludwig hated his lessons intensely.

All through the day, whenever Mr Yewsreddy wasn't paying Ludwig much attention, Ludwig watched the people coming and going into his grandmother's house. First, Sir Notsworth had popped in all dressed and raring to go. Then Hephaestus had left with the Captain, no doubt heading to the docks to check on the *Kamaria*. They returned a few hours later. Pashymore also appeared, looking slightly less angry than he had done the last time Ludwig had seen him. He sidled off with Matilda and Ludwig watched as they spoke in low voices next to the rose bushes at the other end of the garden.

'Ludwig,' said Mr Yewsreddy. 'Pay attention, boy.'

Ludwig turned back to his work but the old man's dull voice made him even more fidgety. He wanted to leave and to be out on the waves finding his father. Stopping whatever was going to happen from happening. He didn't want to be listening to a man telling him things most of which he already knew. But that was it, wasn't it. What *was* happening? Who or what was Grilsgarter? Was it that machine or did the machine belong to someone else called Grilsgarter? And what did he or they want with father? The HELOTs probably, Ludwig guessed. It was the best reason he could come up with. Everyone had seen what they could do. Maybe there would be another attack. Ludwig shuddered. It didn't bear thinking about.

He wondered about other things too. His grandmother had read something in those papers in his father's study, something that scared her and made her burn down the castle, Ludwig was sure of it. But what? She had said it was something about grandfather but that was it. And finally, who was the Painted Man? Both his grandmother and the Captain wouldn't say anything more. Ludwig let out a sigh of annoyance causing Mr Yewsreddy to look at him angrily.

'I do hope I'm not boring you, boy,' said Mr Yewsreddy. 'As I'm the only person who agreed to take you as a pupil you should be more polite in my company.'

'Yes Mr Yewsreddy. Sorry Mr Yewsreddy,' Ludwig said without feeling. The lesson was a waste of time.

'Good. Now, please recite chapter three. I shall be testing you on it tomorrow.'

Around lunch time, Mr Yewsreddy called for a break and Ludwig wandered into the house. Inside, he found Matilda hugging the Captain and Hephaestus. She turned when she heard Ludwig behind her.

'Ah, there you are,' Matilda called out. 'Everyone is ready to go. Do you want to say goodbye?'

Ludwig didn't reply.

'I'll make sure I keep notes,' said Sir Notsworth. 'Maybe this trip will be perfect for the next book. You can read all about it when we get back. How about that?'

Ludwig starred daggers at him. The last thing he wanted

to do was read about it. 'I still want to come with you,' he said sullenly.

'Right...' Sir Notsworth trailed off. He twirled his whiskers nervously and looked at Matilda.

'We've been over this,' said his grandmother firmly.

Hephaestus knelt down in front of his brother. 'I know you're angry, but you saw that machine. You shouldn't have to go up against something like that, especially when we just don't know what's going on. If Beacon is attacked, grandmother can protect you. But we're chasing that thing, Ludwig. Who knows where that's going to lead us.'

Ludwig snorted. 'I don't care, it'd be better than being here. Why are *you* going?'

'I'm needed to look after the ship and the Captain,' Hephaestus replied. 'I have to go, but I don't want to leave you feeling like this.'

'Then take me with you!'

'You know we can't.'

'Come on, mate,' said the Captain. 'You know yer need to sit this one out. That creature'll crush you like a bug if yer got near it, and yer grandmother would never let me forget it if I got you killed.'

Ludwig looked at those gathered. He tried to think of something to say to convince them but nothing would come. Instead, he turned and stalked off towards his grandmother's kitchen to find something to eat.

'Fine. Go then,' he called out over his shoulder.

A short while later, after Ludwig had eaten lunch alone at the kitchen table he walked back out into the garden just in time to see Hephaestus, the Captain, and Sir Notsworth leave. He felt stupid for acting badly but he couldn't help it.

He had to go, no matter what.

Sighing to himself, Ludwig looked over at his tutor. In the far corner of the garden, Mr Yewsreddy was sitting dozing in the sun, his loud snores carried to Ludwig's ears on a gentle breeze. Rather than disturb him, Ludwig sat on the grass and felt in his pocket. The HELOT was there, lying quietly.

'At least you're still here,' he said to the little machine.

On the driveway, carts full of supplies for the *Kamaria* were now getting ready to leave too. Ludwig stared at them for a few moments then, nodding to himself, made up his mind.

I'm coming with you, he thought. Whether you like it or not.

He crept over to the back of the last cart in the line. It was piled high with boxes covered with a tarpaulin and the driver sat at the front looking bored and shouting occasionally to the other cart drivers. Ludwig reached out and pulled the tarpaulin up. Underneath, there was space in between two boxes small enough for a boy of Ludwig's size to hide.

'Too young am I?' Ludwig whispered to the little HELOT. 'I'll show them too young.'

He lifted the corner of his jacket so his ear was as close to his pocket as possible. 'What's that? You think I should climb in there? I don't know... well fine, I will!'

He quickly looked around. No one was watching and no one was nearby except for the driver. Without a second thought, Ludwig dived into the gap between the boxes and pulled the tarpaulin back into place. 'Here we go!' he whispered.

A minute or so passed then there was a shout and the cart pulled away. 'I'll show them,' Ludwig hissed to his unlikely new friend.

The Captain and Hephaestus stood on the dock near to the *Kamaria Pili*, surrounded by workmen and sailors who were getting the ship ready to set sail. Matilda had put word out they were going to hunt for Mandrake as soon as she had returned from Little Wainesford and every able-bodied sailor had turned up at the docks that morning. The Captain had looked each one over and spoken to them in turn. Once those who didn't know difference between port and starboard had been weeded out, he had sat down the rest and told them of the plan: find Mandrake.

However, the Captain decided not to tell them he was mostly a machine. It would only cause problems. A rumour was going around the ship that the Captain had been hurt during the HELOT attack and he wore a steel mask to cover a terrible disfigurement. Seeing that many of his new crew found this idea both impressive and unnerving at the same time, the Captain decided not tell them otherwise. A little bit of awe and fear was good for getting people to take orders.

'Do you think he'll be okay?' asked Hephaestus as the Captain inspected his new crew.

'Sure, mate,' replied the Captain, watching his new hands go about various tasks. 'He'll be grumpy for a few days but he'll be right as rain soon enough. He's a sensible lad.'

'I've never seen him look at me like that.'

'He's goin' to 'ave to learn he can't get his own way all the time. It won't do him any harm. He'll be pleased to see you when you get back and all of this forgotten, you'll see.'

Hephaestus didn't look convinced. 'Where are we heading?' he asked, changing the subject.

'Guly Porta,' replied the Captain. 'The Painted Man is there. It's a couple of months journey west once we're clear of Pallenway as long as the weather holds.'

'I've heard of it.'

'I'm not surprised, a well-read lad like you.'

'It has a certain... reputation.'

'That it has, mate. That it most definitely has.'

Hephaestus decided not to press the matter further. He looked around the docks. 'Where's Sir Notsworth?' he asked.

'I'm not sure,' replied the Captain. 'He ran off as soon as we arrived. He'll be here, don't worry.'

Ludwig was thrown around in every direction as the cart trundled through Beacon's cobbled streets. He felt every bump and hole in the road. One shoulder was now almost numb from the repeated beating it was taking.

After what seemed like a lifetime, the cart came to a stop again. Ludwig quietly huffed with relief and tried to stretch as much as his could without a leg or arm poking out. On the other side of the tarpaulin he heard the cries of seagulls and the shouts of the dockworkers calling to one another. He lifted the sheet slightly and took a peek. He was at Beacon docks.

Nearby, he saw the Captain and Hephaestus talking to each other. Around them others milled about preparing the ship and loading supplies. Then he saw the *Kamaria* itself and nearly gasped. The ship was huge! Ludwig was amazed it was even able to float. He hadn't been down to the docks while Hephaestus had been working and had no idea.

Behind him, Ludwig heard a creak as the driver climbed off the cart. Before the man had unloaded the crates, Ludwig slunk off the back of the cart and darted between the wheels. He watched hidden as the man stood where he'd been only moments before.

'Where d'you want this?' the man called out to someone. His feet were only a few inches from Ludwig, and Ludwig dared not breathe.

'Get a couple o' the hands and unload over there,' Ludwig heard another voice say.

While the crates were being moved, Ludwig sneaked out from under the front of the cart and ran towards another pile of crates and boxes near the ship.

I bet I could hide in one of them, he thought to himself.

When he got to the first crate, he tried the lid but it was nailed down tight. He went to the next but it was the same. Ludwig grunted in annoyance. Now what? His plan was starting to come undone already. It wasn't as if he could just walk on board.

'Hey you!'

Ludwig spun round wide-eyed. He had been spotted. He looked about, desperate to find somewhere to run and hide but he was out of luck. He let his shoulders sag and prepared for his capture and the almost certain shouting that would follow. The Captain was going to have kittens.

Ludwig looked up to see a scruffy-looking boy with short, sandy-coloured hair coming towards him. He looked about the same age as Ludwig, maybe a year or two younger.

'Whatya doin'?' the boy asked.

'Er...' replied Ludwig.

'Come on, out with it.'

'Well–'

The boy looked Ludwig over and winked. 'Hang on, are yer one of the new deckhands?'

Ludwig had no idea what was going on but the boy seemed to want to help him.

'Sure,' said Ludwig. 'That's why I'm here.'

The boy grinned. 'Right you are. You best come with me.' The boy turned and led Ludwig to a group of other boys who were standing around an older man.

Please don't recognise me, Ludwig thought as they

got closer.

'Filo, Ulli,' shouted the older man. 'I want those boxes in the hold in the next five minutes. Get to it.'

The two boys to whom the man had spoken ran off.

'And if you don't get to it right now you'll feel the back of my hand, so you will!' he called after them.

He peered at his clipboard and then at the rest of the boys.

'Senka? Senka! Now where is that brat?'

The man looked up and saw Ludwig and the boy who had found him coming towards him. 'Senka, there you are! And who's that?'

'He's one of us, boss,' said the boy called Senka quickly. He nudged Ludwig sharply in the ribs. 'That's right, ain't it?'

'Yes!' said Ludwig eagerly. He couldn't believe his luck. Could it really be this easy? Would they just let him on board?'

'What's yer name, boy?' said the man, eyeing Ludwig suspiciously. 'I thought we had all the deckhands.'

'Er... Lian... Sir.' replied Ludwig, remembering the name the Captain had given him when he had hidden in his circus all those months ago.

'Well, "Er... Lian", I don't recognise yer.'

'He was with us when yer hired us, boss,' said Senka. 'Weren't yer...'

'Yes– Yeah!' said Ludwig. 'I was here from the start!' Ludwig felt pleased with himself. The man seemed to believe him.

The man stared at Ludwig for a few seconds then said:

'Fine, then yer know the pay and know what yer doin'. You and Senka, grab those boxes for the galley over there. Take 'em on board and find Chef. He'll tell yer where t' stow 'em.'

Senka grabbed Ludwig's sleeve and pulled him away while

the older man looked back at his clipboard.

'That were a close one,' said Senka. 'Thought you were gonna get tol' t' push off.'

'Why did you do that?' asked Ludwig.

'You ain't hangin' around here for fun, are yer?' said Senka as he grabbed one of the smaller boxes piled up nearby. 'I guessed you were lookin' fer work. Azmon knows yer look like yer need it. Yer nothin' but skin and bones. What 'appened? Lost yer dad in the Terror?'

'The Terror?' asked Ludwig as he took a box as well.

'Where 'ave yer bin? Yeah, the Terror, you know, with those machines. The Von Guggenstein Terror.'

That's what they are calling it... thought Ludwig.

'Yeah. Something like that,' he mumbled.

They made their way towards the *Kamaria* and as they came up to the gangplank Ludwig could hear the Captain and Hephaestus. He lifted the box he was carrying so it covered his face and hoped they wouldn't notice him.

'I hear yer,' said Senka while Ludwig hid. 'I lost mine before then, but Azmon knows there are plenty without a mum and dad after the Terror. By the look of it yours were well off at least. Fancy clothes you got there.'

When they were on the *Kamaria's* deck Ludwig looked down at himself. He was wearing clothes his grandmother had bought him. He guessed they were good. He'd never really thought about it before. 'They... they did all right.'

'But they're gone now, eh?' said Senka.

'I guess.'

Ludwig followed Senka down a hatch on deck into the belly of the ship. He remembered the last time he had been on a boat and shuddered. Ludwig had been kept for days in a small cage with only a couple of mute HELOTs for company while Jack, his father's slave, stalked the deck above him.

'Well, what's past is past,' continued Senka. 'Can't get

'em back.'

'No, I suppose not.' Ludwig wanted to change the subject. 'What does a deck hand do?'

'Skivvying mostly,' explained Senka, 'but don't worry, it's a better job than most. Explorin' the seas, visitin' strange places! You help out around the ship where yer needed. Many o' the sailors on board learnt their trade as deckhands. An' this time we're doin' something special. We're goin' after Mandrake himself! Imagine that! We'll be heroes when we get 'im!'

'That'll be good,' said Ludwig. It was all he could think to say out loud. What he wanted to say was: don't you remember what happened last time? He took over Beacon and no one could stop him! If it weren't for me, thousands would have died in the fighting! It won't be *that* easy.

Ludwig followed Senka further and further down into the *Kamaria*. Finally they entered a long corridor that appeared to stretch the length of the ship and stopped by a door about half way along it. Through the door, Ludwig spied pots and pans and things bubbling on gimballed stoves, filling the air with rich aromas and making Ludwig's stomach rumble. They were in the galley.

In the middle of the room was a thin, pale-looking man dressed in white busily chopping a pile of vegetables on a sturdy-looking table. He looked up when Ludwig and Senka came in.

'All right, Chef?' Senka called out.

The man looked up and a smile spread across his face. 'Senka? Is that you?' He put down his knife and peered. 'Why, it is you. I haven't seen you for a while.'

'You neither, Chef. Keepin' well?'

'Can't complain, can't complain,' said Chef, waving his hand vaguely. 'What have you got there?'

'This is Lian,' replied Senka. 'He's a new deckhand.'

'Hello, Lian,' said Chef. He paused and looked at Ludwig

for a short while then said: 'However Senka, while it is a pleasure to make the acquaintance of this young gentleman, I was in fact referring to those boxes in your arms.'

'Oh, right. Your supplies. Bert sent 'em.'

'Ah, good. Put them over there if you'd be so kind.'

Chef pointed and Ludwig and Senka went over to the other side of the room. They dropped their boxes in a small alcove that served as a pantry.

'You'll get on with Chef,' whispered Senka. 'He's educated too. Dunno what he's doin' sailin' but no one dare ask him. Someone did once and next day 'e turned up dead with a fishbone in 'is throat. Those in charge said were an accident but us lot know better.' He winked at Ludwig.

'Are you two free?' called Chef as the boys turned to leave.

'We could be,' said Senka. 'Why?'

'I could do with a hand down here.' Chef looked at Ludwig. 'Do you know how to cook, boy?'

Back in Little Wainesford Ludwig had helped Mrs Pewsnitt, his father's housekeeper, in the kitchen a few times. She had taught Ludwig a thing or two. 'Yes,' he said. 'A bit.'

'Good, that's more than Senka then. You can show him how to do it. Grab some aprons and we'll get started, and I'll even tell you about how Senka nearly poisoned the Captain of the *Sea Plough*. I don't think there's a man alive brave enough to face Senka's stew after that.'

Ludwig couldn't help but laugh.

'Hey!' said Senka. 'How were I t' know you weren't meant to use those bits o' the jellyfish. You never tol' me not to!'

Chef sighed.

'Most people know the stingers are something to avoid,' he replied as the boys grabbed an apron. Then he handed them a knife each. 'Right, you can start with dinner tonight. This—' he explained to Senka, speaking slowly while winking at Ludwig, '– is a knife. Lian, show him how to use it without cutting his fingers off will you?'

'What ho!'

Hephaestus looked up to see Sir Notsworth walking along the dock. He was dressed in his explorer's uniform complete with wide-brimmed hat and khaki shirt and shorts. He had a hunting rifle over his shoulder which he was patting affectionately. Behind him, Hephaestus recognised Sir Notsworth's "companions"; a group of people the explorer had employed over the years to help him in his adventures. However, Hephaestus noticed that there were quite a few new faces in the crowd.

'Not gone without us, eh?' Sir Notsworth called out.

Hephaestus caught the Captain's eye. He was sure if the Captain was capable of facial expressions he would be grimacing right now.

'What are they doin' here?' asked the Captain, nodding towards the companions. 'I don't remember agreein' to 'ave 'em along. You: no problem. Them: no.'

'Well I couldn't leave them behind could I?' said Sir Notsworth, looking very hurt. 'Going off to save Pallenway and what-not. They'd be terribly upset and I'd never hear the end of it.'

Hephaestus looked at the companions. They were a group of men and women so bizarre and fearsome he doubted they'd ever been upset over anything. Angry? Yes, to the point where they'd cut bits off of you for looking at them funny, but not upset.

'I don't recognise some of them,' said Hephaestus.

'Ah, quite a few of them were busy when you and Ludwig last visited. Helping out against the HELOTs and similar.'

'We have enough men already,' said the Captain flatly.

Sir Notsworth grabbed the arm of one man who was almost as big as Hephaestus. He looked like he could uproot a forest with his bare hands. 'But Captain, Killer here was devastated when he thought I was going without him. Weren't you Killer?' said Sir Notsworth, patting the huge man's arm. 'Nearly cried, so he did.'

There was a snigger from the other companions that Sir Notsworth appeared not to hear. Also, Hephaestus noticed that "Killer" didn't look too pleased at what Sir Notsworth was saying. His knuckles were cracking for a start.

'I weren't cryin'' said Killer.

'No, no, of course you weren't, my man,' said Sir Notsworth, giving Hephaestus and the Captain a sly look. 'But you weren't too happy, were you?'

Killer shrugged then shook his head. 'Suppose not.'

'Look at that face, Captain,' said Sir Notsworth. How could you say "no" to that?'

The Captain and Hephaestus looked at that face and that face looked back. Saying "no" to it would have been difficult, no doubt.

'All right, mate,' said the Captain. 'But you pay 'em and keep 'em in line. Any trouble and we'll leave them on the first island we come to, understand? And they'll be sleeping in the crew's quarters.'

'Not a problem,' replied Sir Notsworth. He turned round to another Companion. 'Gu'Liok, take everyone below and see they are quartered.'

A strange little fat man covered in silk robes that swished when he walked sidled up to Sir Notsworth.

'Yesss, sir,' said the man who was called Gu'Liok. He turned to the other Companions. 'Come.'

Sir Notsworth mopped his brow as he watched them walk up the gangplank.

'Interesting man, that. I met Gu'Liok in Ferristainez a couple of years ago. Can't do without him now. Oh no. Like family. Saw him kill ten men with a hairbrush once. Not entirely sure why since there were perfectly good swords lying about, but still very impressive. I think he wanted to show off. Now, a game of shuffle-board might be in order I think.'

Sir Notsworth pulled a piece of chalk out of one of his numerous pockets. 'Where can I draw the court? Killer beat me last time and I need to win my money back. Doesn't look it does he, but he's a dab hand at the sport and no mistake.'

The Captain and Hephaestus looked at one another as Sir Notsworth boarded the ship.

'You're workin' your passage!' The Captain called after him. 'This ain't a cruise ship, remember that!' He looked back at Hephaestus. 'This could be a long journey,' he grumbled.

Hephaestus let out a snort that could have been a laugh. A few minutes later, the gangplank was pulled up and stowed away. The Captain called out to the dockworkers and the moorings were loosened and pulled back up into the ship. The *Kamaria Pili* was ready to leave.

The Captain walked over to the ship's wheel and, with a nod to his first mate, he turned the wheel and the ship headed out to sea.

Chapter Eight:
Beacon Intrigues

Back in Beacon things were not as they should be.

'Pashymore!' Matilda cried, banging on the thick wooden door to the Councillor's office deep within the council chambers. 'If you don't let me in right now I'll skin you alive you horrible little man!'

It was the day after the *Kamaria* had set sail and Matilda von Guggenstein had learned that Ludwig was no longer in her mansion nor under her care. After screaming and shouting at her staff for some time, she jumped in her carriage and headed straight for Beacon's centre. At this precise moment she was standing in Pashymore's office and her anger was rising even further. In front of her was the Councillor's personal secretary; a fussy, officious man seemingly bred specifically for government work, and he was getting in her way.

'Madam, I assure you,' said the secretary, 'Councillor Pashymore will see you as soon as it is convenient. He is in a meeting right now but if you'd like to wait–'

'Wait?' shouted Matilda. 'How dare you!'

'Please, madam–' the secretary continued, but he was interrupted by the creaking of Pashymore's office door. It appeared the Councillor's meeting had finished.

Matilda shook the secretary's grasping hand from her sleeve and was about to storm into Pashymore's office when two evil-looking men blocked her entrance. They were huge, with long oily hair and scarred faces and arms. They took up the door-frame and stared at Matilda in sneering curiosity until she stepped out of their way. One gave a short laugh and whispered something to his partner, and his partner grinned evilly as they passed her and left the office. Matilda watched them go before rushing into the office without the secretary stopping her. She slammed the door behind her.

Pashymore looked up from some paperwork on his desk. 'Matilda, so it was you making all that racket outside. Was it really necessary?'

Matilda eyes were wide. 'Harold!' she shouted. 'Ludwig's gone!'

Pashymore put his pen down and stared at Matilda. 'What do you mean: gone?'

'What do you think I mean? I can't find him anywhere!' replied Matilda. 'I know he goes off on his own sometimes but his teacher said he never came back to his lessons yesterday, and he didn't come home last night either. I'm sick with worry! What if– if he's been taken?'

Matilda walked forward and dropped into one of the chairs in front of Pashymore's desk. Despite herself, she noticed the smell of unwashed people. She guessed it must be from the two men who had been to see Pashymore before her.

'I think you would have known about it if he had,' replied Pashymore calmly. 'Someone would have seen something. Mandrake seems to have a flare for the dramatic and this doesn't seem like him. Besides, didn't the Captain leave yesterday? I bet Ludwig's with him.'

Matilda sagged. 'In all honesty the possibility occurred to me too. As far as I can tell he disappeared at the same time as the *Kamaria* left and the last anyone saw him was when we all said goodbye. But after all that has happened I can't help but fear the worst.' She appeared more calm now.

'But we can't take chances,' said Pashymore. 'I'll get word out to the city watch to keep a look out in case he's still here. Security is tight after what happened in Nikolis Square.'

Councillor Pashymore went to his office door and opened

it. He issued some orders to his secretary and then returned to his desk. 'I'll let you know if we hear anything,' he said to Matilda.

'Thank you.' Matilda stood up, turned, and was about to leave when a thought occurred to her. 'Harold, who were those men?'

'It's of no importance Matilda,' said Pashymore not looking up from his paperwork.

'Harold, you didn't...'

'Don't look at me like that. Your son is a menace and while you put a great deal of faith in this Captain of yours, personally I don't trust a man who won't even give you his real name. Those gentlemen will make every effort to bring Mandrake to justice. I've promised them a great deal of money if they do.'

'But bounty hunters?'

'I know they can be risky but I've had some success with them in the past. There's no one in our army suitable for a job like this and I need all my men here to make sure the city doesn't descend into chaos. I simply cannot have your son running about free to do as he likes, so they are the best solution.'

'They can cause more problems than they are worth.'

'I know but did you see the streets today?'

Matilda had not been paying attention when she had travelled to the council chambers, but she had to admit the journey appeared to have been quicker than usual.

'Hardly anyone left their home today,' said Pashymore. 'And farmers aren't bringing their goods to the city either. Beacon is dying out of fear, Matilda. They're terrified Mandrake will be back.'

Matilda looked at the Councillor and nodded. 'I understand Harold, but if Ludwig gets hurt because of them...'

'I will tell them to bring Ludwig back if they find him, how about that? His safety is assured if they do run into him.'

'Very well, but if anything happens things will not go well for you.' She went to the door and opened it.

'Right now I'm not sure how things could be worse,' Pashymore replied. 'Trust me, Matilda, Ludwig will turn up perfectly well, you'll see.'

Chapter Nine:
Setting Sail

During the first few days on board the *Kamaria*, Ludwig was told in no uncertain terms that the deckhands were not to be seen if at all possible. Rather than clutter the corridors of the ship, the hands had their own rabbit warren of tunnels they could use to go back and forth. Most of these tunnels were high enough for the younger boys to stand up in, but the older ones (including Ludwig), had to bend down to avoid banging their heads. Unfortunately some of the tunnels were so small that even the younger boys had to crawl on hands and feet in order to get from one place to the next. However, while these tunnels weren't comfortable to use, it did mean Ludwig could move about without fear of anyone who knew him recognising him.

Ludwig quickly learnt the deckhands were there to help out whenever they were called. They lived in one corner of the hold where along one wall was a row of bells and whenever a bell rang, a boy had to run to whoever had called. One of the bells had *"The Captain"* written below it and Ludwig dreaded it ringing in case no one else was there and he would have to go himself.

'Don't worry,' said Senka when he saw Ludwig looking at the bell. 'It hardly ever rings. Besides, it'll be one of the more experienced boys who go. The new 'uns are given the worst jobs. You'll be in the bilge and the galley more often than not.'

Ludwig and the other boys stayed in the hold when they weren't working, using the pile of blankets they had been given to make small nests for themselves to sleep in, or they would go to one of the lesser used tunnels to be alone and have some time to themselves. When Ludwig wasn't in the galley helping Chef, he found himself sitting in his nest or one of the tunnels with Senka and listen to Senka's sailing stories.

However Ludwig, as much as he hated to admit it, started to think this "adventure" was not such a good idea. Despite the *Kamaria* being new, which meant the boys weren't sharing their home with rats and spiders, and despite the other boys being friendly enough, Ludwig had begun to feel down.

Being on the ship was hard work, and with the bells ringing at all hours it was hard to sleep. What was worse was how alone he felt. He knew his brother was just above him, but he could have been a million miles away as far as Ludwig was concerned. He had even, in the darker moments during the first few days of the voyage, thought about perhaps owning up to being on board. But then he would picture the Captain and imagine what he would say, and Ludwig decided to stay hidden a while longer at least. It wasn't that bad, and getting shouted at was unlikely to cheer him up.

In order to occupy himself while he dozed in his nest in the evenings, Ludwig got the other boys to share stories of their voyages or, from those that had not sailed before, what happened to their families during the Terror.

The seasoned sailors in the group had been orphans before the Terror and had been deckhands for years. They told of the places they had visited and the ships they served on; the captains that had beaten them or treated them well; of treasure and of friends lost to shipwrecks, pirates, or disease. The oldest must have been sixteen, the youngest was about six.

The "new 'uns", as Senka and the others called all those who had never been a deckhand before, told of the HELOTs breaking into their homes and taking their parents while they hid and watched through cracks and peep-holes. Ludwig felt terrible every time they spoke, but he wanted to hear everything anyway. At one point Senka had even tried to get Ludwig to tell them what had happened to his parents, but Ludwig had kept quiet. He couldn't tell them the truth, but he really didn't want to lie. He'd done enough deceiving already.

Ludwig also realised this was the first time he had really spent time with people of his own age. There had been school in Greater Wainesford, a few miles away from Ludwig's village where some of the other children from Little Wainesford went. However Ludwig had been taught by his father instead and kept at home. He had always been around adults pretty much all his life. This was all very new.

Yet despite the miserable stories, the lack of sleep, and the long working hours, at times Ludwig found himself having quite a bit of fun. When he worked in the kitchens, Chef had begun teaching him to cook all sorts of dishes from the creatures the sailors had dragged from the seas and from the goods in the ship's stores. The food Chef prepared was incredible, and Ludwig doubted he'd eaten better even in the palace in Galleesha or his own grandmother's mansion. On one occasion, a Fulsome Kippering had been caught and rather than throw the body back out to sea, Chef insisted it was brought to the galley. Fulsome Kipperings are seven feet long with hides so thick harpoons cannot pierce it, and known to be the most evil-tasting fish in existence. Ludwig was shown how to make a meal fit for a Superbus from it. The crew had even wanted seconds.

A week or so into the voyage, there was a bump that meant the ship had docked somewhere. Ludwig looked up from the stew he was cooking to see Senka standing at the galley door.

'We're at Okla,' said Senka. 'Most ships sailin' across the ocean to Guly Porta and such stop 'ere for last minute supplies. It's a long trip from now on.'

Ludwig noticed Senka had a basket full of letters in his hand. 'What's that?' he asked.

'For Beacon,' explained Senka. 'Last chance to send post back home.'

'Wait,' said Ludwig. 'Do you have any paper and pencils?'

Senka rummaged in the basket, pulled out a pencil and paper and handed them to Ludwig. 'Be quick,' he said. 'We're leavin' soon and I don't want t' be left 'ere.'

Ludwig wiped the food from his hands on his apron, and then took the pencil and wrote:

Grandmother,

I'm sorry for running off but I had to help find father. I hope you understand and are not too angry with me. I am safe and well.

I love you and will be home soon.

Ludwig.

He folded the paper, wrote his grandmother's address on the outside and dropped it in the letter basket. He had addressed the letter to "grandmother" only rather than Matilda von Guggenstein in case Senka should happen to notice.

'Thanks,' said Ludwig. Senka nodded and left.

Chapter Ten:
Port of Call

After about a month and a half of sailing, Ludwig woke in his nest to find the other deckhands milling about excitedly.

'We're here!' Senka called out.

Ludwig stowed his blankets and ran out of the hold. He, Senka and the other deckhands ran through the tunnels and stairwell that led to the deck, but when they got near, Ludwig was careful not to make himself visible to anyone who might recognise him. He peeked out from one of the hatches and spotted Hephaestus and the Captain.

'Weigh anchor, mates,' the Captain called out. 'Hephaestus an' I will head out later when night falls. Everyone else is to stay 'ere until we know what's goin' on.'

Ludwig disappeared below deck again and bided his time.

Once the crew had departed, Hephaestus, standing on deck, tied off the rope he was holding and looked up, shading his eyes from the sun. Over the shimmering blue water he saw the small town of Guly Porta perched on the edge of the sea. Occasionally, he heard a noise that he could have sworn was a gun shot. The Captain was nearby. Everyone else had gone below decks for supper.

'Was that what I think it was?' asked Hephaestus.

'Aye, mate,' replied the Captain. 'Guly Porta is a interestin' place, mainly 'cus people seem to spend most of their time tryin' to shoot one another.'

'Why?'

'There's not much in the way of law there,' explained the Captain. 'So everyone is armed and deals out "justice" themselves.'

'It sounds crazy.'

'It is. You have to be quick and careful if yer goin' to survive.'

'You sound like you lived there yourself.'

'I did, mate. Fifteen years.'

Hephaestus looked wide-eyed at the Captain. 'And you're still alive?'

'Just about.'

'Why are we waiting to go over there?' Hephaestus asked.

'The Painted Man won't be around until the evening,' said the Captain. 'I've never known him to be out when the sun is up.'

'How do you know him?'

'Well, you know how you regret ever comin' up with those HELOTs?'

Hephaestus looked surprised. 'What?'

'Don't be shocked, mate. We all know. All yer've been doin' is work. Yer barely talk to anyone any more. Yer blame yerself for 'em, I'm guessin'. But yer can't torture yerself like that, it ain't healthy.'

Hephaestus gritted his teeth. He hated hearing the "H" word.

'It's all that matters to anyone any more,' Hephaestus rumbled. 'No one talks about anything else.'

'It'll pass, you'll see.'

'Maybe.'

'All that anger jus' knotted up inside yer because of 'em, you feel it?' Hephaestus nodded his head. 'The Painted Man is the one who's done that to me,' said the Captain. 'He's someone I wish I never had anythin' to do with.'

'Why?'

'I used t' work fer 'im, and I did some terrible things. You know what I used to do before I met yer Grandmother?'

'Gill had said something about it,' said Hephaestus. Gill had worked in the Captain's circus when Hephaestus and Ludwig had been taken there after running away from home. He had said the Captain had been a *"re-distributor of sea-going goods"*; in other words: a pirate.

'It's a time in my life I'm not proud of, and much of it's because of the Painted Man. He's cruel and he's devious, and if he knows anything about Mandrake or this Grilsgarter, it'll cost us dear.'

Hephaestus looked at the Captain sadly. 'I understand. Where do we find him?'

'He'll be in *The Jester's Revenge*. It's a tavern in town and he owns it along with everyone in it–' The Captain suddenly went quiet. He looked at Hephaestus and put his finger to his mouth. *Quiet.*

What? mouthed Hephaestus.

The Captain pointed towards one of the hatches that led to the bowels of the ship. He walked over to it slowly, and then threw the hatch cover open. No one was there.

'I could have sworn I heard something,' said the Captain. He looked at Hephaestus. ' No matter. Come on, you must be hungry. Let's eat.'

Chapter Eleven:
The Jester's Revenge

When night fell, Ludwig slunk outside. He waited until the other deckhands were either working somewhere else or asleep and then tip-toed out of the hold, through the tunnels, and finally through one of the many hatches that led out from below.

The air was hot and sweaty being this far south and it was dark on deck. Only a few lanterns hung here and there casting more shadows than light. A couple of Sir Notsworth's Companions were sitting with a few of the crew playing cards and trading stories near the prow, but otherwise the ship was quiet. The only other noise was from the buzzing insects and the sound of the crew grumbling and slapping themselves as they tried to stop the little bloodsuckers eating them alive.

Ludwig stayed low and crept towards the gangplank. He peered over the side of the ship and saw what must be Guly Porta across the water. His heart sank. Rather than tie up at the docks, the Captain had left the ship anchored some distance away. He'd have to swim. Ludwig looked across the ship and saw no longboats had been launched. At least the Captain and Hephaestus hadn't left yet.

He then cast his gaze along the hull and spied the anchor chain close to the prow, not too far away from those playing cards. Grimacing at what he knew he must do, he made his way over to it, staying low and shuffling in the dark. When he was close to the men, he pushed his back against the side of the ship and carried on, hoping it was dark enough for them not to notice him.

Eventually, when he reached the anchor chain, he followed

it to where it left the ship. Then he swung his legs over the side and slowly climbed down. When he touched the cold iron links, he shivered; and about a quarter of the way he froze as a sound rang out from the town.

Was that a gunshot? Where are we?

He waited to see if anything more would happen. But the shot had sounded as if it was from the town and finally, satisfied he wasn't being shot at, Ludwig gritted his teeth and edged closer still to the pitch black sea. The chain links soon became wet and covered in slime. He wanted to jump; to get it over and done with, but he was worried the splash would attract attention so instead he closed his eyes and continued as he had started. Soon enough he felt the lapping of the sea and water pouring into his shoes. He let his legs unwrap from the chain and he dangled them in the sea. Making sure he made no noise, he lowered himself into the cold water. Freezing, Ludwig slowly swam away from the *Kamaria* and towards dry land, wishing all the while the Captain had left the ship much, much closer to shore.

When Ludwig had almost arrived at the town, the Captain appeared on deck with Hephaestus behind him. 'You lot,' the Captain called out to those on deck. 'Get a boat ready. We're leaving.'

The men who had been playing cards got up and went over to the winches next to one of the longboats.

'You sure I should come along?' said Hephaestus.

'When it comes to the Painted Man, there's no one else here I trust.'

'What about Sir Notsworth?'

'Sir Notsworth has his qualities mate, but I think he'll be out of his depth here and might even do something to cause problems. Someone might even try to kidnap him too. He's worth a few coins and a lot of people could recognise that mug of his. I don't want to have to put our search for your father on hold while we go and get him.'

Hephaestus nodded but he wasn't keen on going to Guly Porta. From his cabin he had heard the faint sound of gunshots all through the evening.

'Just don't tell yer grandmother, okay?' said the Captain. 'She'll only fret.'

'Of course,' said Hephaestus.

There was a splash on one side of the *Kamaria* as a longboat hit the water. A rope ladder was thrown over the side and four of the crew went down. The Captain and Hephaestus followed.

'And try not to get shot,' said the Captain when they were safely in the little boat. 'I don't want to have to explain that either.'

It took Ludwig maybe ten minutes to get to Guly Porta. He dragged himself out of the water and gasped. He couldn't stop shivering. He squeezed the water from his clothes and tried to keep his teeth from chattering, worried someone might hear. He rubbed his arms and realised he could barely feel his hands and feet. He quickly looked around and found himself on a small beach near to Guly Porta's wharf where smaller ships were moored up for the evening. No one seemed to be about. Nearby, a few lamps had been lit. He ran over to one and held his hands to it, letting the slight warmth wash over them.

When he felt up to it, he darted over to a stack of lobster traps near one of the piers and hid. He peered out and waited. Soon enough he caught sight of the Captain and Hephaestus.

They were dressed in long, loose, hooded cloaks and when they got off the boat and Ludwig heard them speaking to one another in low voices as they made their way into town. Ludwig followed them, feeling slightly jealous of how well they seemed to be getting on these days.

As Ludwig followed the Captain and Hephaestus, another figure appeared on the deck of the *Kamaria*. It too slipped down the anchor chain and into the black water, and then made its way to the same beach Ludwig had come to. The figure slipped into the town without pausing.

The Captain led Hephaestus down the narrow streets until they reached an ugly, squat building that seemed to be sweating in the heat: *The Jester's Revenge.*

As they made their way through Guly Porta Hephaestus had witnessed dozens of fights and duels. It was as if everyone here was out to do someone else harm. A few had even tried to pick fights with Hephaestus and the Captain, but quickly changed their minds once they realised how big Hephaestus was and went to find someone else more interesting to quarrel with.

The Jester's Revenge stood in a grim, broken-down part of Guly Porta, but Hephaestus noticed that for some reason there seemed to be less fighting here. In the rest of the town, when fights broke out perhaps someone would be left with a broken nose or finger or a toe shot off, but here Hephaestus guessed they played for keeps. Those that walked about were wrapped in long cloaks and kept their hands hidden. It was all very... polite. The buildings themselves reared their backs like startled cats and murk-light shone through windows, staining the ground between tired street lamps that flickered weakly.

By the door to *The Jester's Revenge* was a battered sign showing a man dressed in a bright costume tiptoeing with a long, evil-looking knife in his hand. Hephaestus was wishing more than ever Sir Notsworth had come instead.

'Watch yerself, yer hear?' said the Captain, pushing open the door. 'It ain't safe here. Just stay with me and don't speak.'

Hephaestus nodded and followed the Captain. Beyond, *The Jester's Revenge* hit him like a hammer to the face. The room he found himself in was full of hunched figures crowing at each other over jars full of filthy-looking liquid. They chattered incessantly in a way which was both loud and hushed at the same time; a sickening muffled roar that pressed on Hephaestus' ears making him feel dizzy and sick. Even the air seemed dirty.

As they made their way through the tables, those sitting would look up briefly, curious to know who had disturbed them, but otherwise they were ignored. To one side of the open room was a long bar where more men and a few women sat speaking to one another and ordering drinks. At the very back there was an archway with a curtain drawn across it. The Captain nudged Hephaestus and pointed at the curtain.

'He's through there.'

The Captain pushed the curtain to one side and went through to the next room. Hephaestus did the same. Hephaestus noticed the room they had just walked through had gone completely silent.

On the other side of the curtain, Hephaestus found himself in a small chamber with one round table sitting in the middle of the room surrounded by men. One of the men was a strange sight. He was gnarled and ancient and covered in jewels and tattoos. Almost every patch of skin on show had a mark of some kind or another upon it. Bizarre swirling shapes like the Captain had when he was human, or jewelled precious metals that looked like they had been melted on, adding to the patterns' hypnotism. The only clothes he wore was an expensive looking waist-coat with a gold watch hanging from it and a pair of trousers.

The Painted Man, Hephaestus thought.

The other men sitting with him looked mean and were laughing and jeering to one another as the Captain walked up to the table. When one of the Painted Man's men saw the Captain he stood up and put his hand on the Captain's chest.

'You got an appointment?' the man grunted.

'No,' said the Captain.

'Then yer'd best turn around before yer get hurt,' said the man. He lent forward to see into the darkness of the Captain's hood. 'Hey, what's wrong with yer face?' he continued, reaching for a knife in his belt.

The Captain took one look at the man and then took his hand and twisted. The man shrieked and fell to the floor holding his crumpled fingers. The Captain turned to the table. 'I ain't got time fer this.'

The others went to get up but the strange man stopped them. 'Wait,' he called out, waving them back. He looked at the Captain and Hephaestus and smiled, showing two rows of jewel-encrusted teeth. 'Well this is a surprise,' he laughed. He stood up. 'You'd better come with me. It looks like we've business to attend.'

Another man spoke.

'You sure, boss?'

The back room suddenly went as silent as the front and those on the other side of the curtain sounded as if they had all drawn breath at once.

Hephaestus had a feeling something terrible was about to happen. He watched as the Painted Man slithered around the table and stood over the man who had spoken. The Painted Man placed his hands on the man's shoulders and bent low. Those seated next to the man edged away slightly and their eyes were firmly fixed on the floor.

'Dear Olivre,' said the Painted Man. 'Tut, tut.'

'S– Sorry, sir,' said the man. Hephaestus could see he'd gone very, very pale.

'Ah, you are sorry are you?' said the Painted Man. 'Good. That's something at least.'

'Hurry this up,' said the Captain. 'I don't need the theatrics.'

The Painted Man looked up at the Captain. The smile had not left his lips. 'Impatient aren't we? So be it. Olivre, I shall speak to you afterwards. Please wait here.'

The Painted Man left Olivre shaking in his chair and made his way to a staircase nearby. 'This way, this way,' he called to Hephaestus and the Captain, and they made their way towards him.

When they got to the stairs, Hephaestus turned back. The man called Olivre jumped up and tried to run out of the room, but those next to him grabbed him and held him tight. They threw him across the table and just before Hephaestus had gone too far to see anything further, two of the men pulled out coils of rope.

'He said *"wait"*, Olivre,' said one of the other men. 'We're sorry about this, we really are. We did tell you, you have to admit. We really did tell you.'

This town is insane, Ludwig thought to himself.

He had tried to keep up with his brother and the Captain as much as possible but every few minutes he found himself having to run away from some madman hell-bent on trying to hurt him. What was wrong with these people? This never happened, even in Beacon! Thankfully, no one had caught him... yet.

Panting, Ludwig found himself hiding in an alley and managed to catch sight of the Captain and Hephaestus disappearing inside a building. It looked like an inn and he knew he wouldn't be able to follow them inside (he had tried to get into the *Lantern and Parapet* in Little Wainesford once and had been marched straight back home). But he had to see what was going on.

In the alley he found an empty barrel lying on its side. He pulled it up, put it against tavern wall and climbed onto it. Near his head was a thin strip of glass. He looked through, the barrel creaking worryingly beneath him. The window itself was covered in grime and Ludwig rubbed it, but even then he could only just make out what was on the other side. Hephaestus and the Captain were in a room speaking to another man Ludwig couldn't quite see. Then he saw them leave and a man was thrown over the table. Two other men started to tie him down... Ludwig turned away, not wanting to see what happened next. He doubted it was going to be nice.

This town is insane! he thought again.

He jumped off the barrel and knew one thing: he had to get upstairs. He had to know what was being said. But as far as he could see there was no way he'd make it from here. He looked towards the end of the alley. It was almost pitch black and a little moonlight managed to slide in between the buildings. He remembered walking through his father's cellars when he had been looking for Hephaestus. This felt very similar except this time he was in a town on the other side of the world full of people who seemed very determined to kill anyone they saw! Ludwig wished he was back in the cellar. Right now, he'd happily live down there if it meant he never had to set foot in this town again.

Steeling himself, Ludwig walked forward. He held out his hands, feeling the wall beside him and hoping there would be a stairwell or something that could get him to the upper rooms. Beacon was full of them so maybe this place would be too. He edged onwards, but when he reached out further his hand brushed against something soft.

'You ain't from around here, are yer?' came a voice from the dark.

On the first floor of *The Jester's Revenge* the Captain and Hephaestus followed the Painted Man through a door into a small room. Inside were a few richly padded chairs facing one another and a fire was burning in the grate despite the heat of the evening.

'Sit, sit,' said the Painted Man. He stoked the fire and waited for Hephaestus and the Captain to take their seats before he did. 'Drinks? Food?' he asked.

Hephaestus and the Captain shook their heads.

'You can remove those hoods now, yes?' said the Painted Man. The Captain and Hephaestus pulled down their hoods and the Painted Man whistled.

'Ah, so *you* must be Hephaestus von Guggenstein. I've heard a great deal about you, young man. It is an honour.'

The Painted Man's eyes then slid along the lines that patterned the Captain's metal face. 'And if it isn't my old friend Captain Tom, albeit looking quite different these days? But that can't be right. A little mouse told me you'd died...'

'I'm still 'ere,' replied the Captain. 'Alive an' kickin', in my own way.' Hephaestus had a feeling the Captain would have been biting his tongue if he had one.

'So you are! So you are!' said the Painted Man, clapping.

'And what happened, Captain? Come, you can tell little old me. Whisper it into my ear.' The Painted Man leaned forward and turned his head.

'I think you already know.'

'Oh, I've heard rumours, to be sure. Some accident or other that left you without a face? Wasn't that it?'

Hephaestus shifted uncomfortably in his chair. How could the Painted Man have known? Those rumours had been started only a few days before the *Kamaria* had set sail. He also felt like there was something going on here he didn't understand. The Painted Man then turned to him.

'Apologies Hephaestus. When two old friends meet, you know how it is... or, well, maybe not if what I've heard is true. Locked up down there all in the dark, were you not? Such a shame, such a great shame. People can be so cruel.'

'How–?' began Hephaestus, but his question was waved away by the Painted Man.

'I imagine the Captain hasn't bothered to explain what I do. He always did keep his cards close to his chest. No matter. Perhaps another little demonstration will help.' The Painted Man rose, walked to deep cabinet behind his chair and opened it.

'*No...*' whispered Hephaestus what he caught sight of the cabinet's contents.

Inside was a HELOT, or at least what had once been one. It was sitting down like a rag doll and it had been pulled apart; its insides laid jumbled up around its feet as if gutted.

'You've got one?' said Hephaestus, horrified.

'Of course!' said the Painted Man. 'It wasn't difficult. There's quite a market for them... or so I've heard. I've a buyer for this one already.'

Hephaestus tensed his hands and the arms of the chair started to crack.

'Stay in control, mate,' whispered the Captain.

'You wouldn't believe how much they are willing to pay,' the Painted Man continued. 'You and I know it's useless of course.' He reached into a pocket and held up a small metal cube. Hephaestus recognised it immediately. It was one of the cubes that held the minds of the people his father had used to make the HELOTs work. 'This is the key, isn't it?' said the Painted Man. 'Don't worry, I won't be selling this. However, it wouldn't matter if I did. These HELOTs are quite useless, but I avoid telling people that. I know only one man holds the secret to their creation.'

Not one, thought Hephaestus. He turned and looked at the Captain. 'This can't be true.'

'Sorry, mate,' replied the Captain. 'He's right. People were sellin' 'em to the highest bidder as soon as they stopped workin'. Pashymore tried to stop 'em but it were impossible.'

'But HELOTs again? In the hands of people like him?' Hephaestus nodded towards their host.

The Painted Man crossed his hands over his heart. 'That hurts. I am merely a trader, nothing more. That is my job. I buy; I sell, anything and everything. People have dreams and, more importantly, they have money. I'm happy to help them with their desires for a fee. I have no ambition beyond that. So I keep my eyes and ears open, I pick up bits and pieces here and there. You'd be amazed what some people will pay for.'

'This isn't why we're here,' interrupted the Captain.

'Well maybe it is and maybe it isn't. As I said, no one knows how to make the HELOTs work or build new ones, except for one person, yes? You're here about Mandrake's disappearance I presume. This is something I might be able to help you with.'

'How could you know?' rumbled Hephaestus, getting annoyed at how well informed this awful man was. 'We set sail only a week—' He stopped when his felt the Captain's arm on his own.

'Easy, mate.' The Captain turned to the Painted Man. 'Aye, that's why we're here. We know you had dealings between Mandrake and someone called Grilsgarter. What do you know?'

The Painted Man laughed. 'Captain, my captain, you flatter me! I may know a thing or two, yes, but what's it worth? That's the question.'

The Captain spoke without hesitation. 'One year. That's it, nothing more. I'll come to you as soon as this is finished.'

'My, you are keen! A year, you say? Well, that is tempting. Oh, how I've missed you, Captain. A year you say? That is a very long time. We could do so much together. Well, let me think... ah, sold!'

Hephaestus lent over to the Captain. 'What have you just done?'

'I did what's needed, mate, that's all. He wouldn't take anything less.'

Hephaestus looked at the Captain. He guessed this had cost his friend a great deal. Hephaestus could only guess at the life to which he was prepared to return in order to get Mandrake back.

'Your turn,' said the Captain.

'Mandrake von Guggenstein was kidnapped,' said the Painted Man.

'Kidnapped?' said Hephaestus, shocked. 'Not rescued?'

'Indeed. There have been rumours... whisperings... that a ship was needed to sail to Beacon and back again. A ship for a contact of mine: one Aliester Grilsgarter. Destined for Beacon. I have passed correspondence between him and your father and you should know, from what I can tell, Grilsgarter and Mandrake are not friends. If Grilsgarter took Mandrake, it was certainly not out of a desire to help him.'

'Who is Aliester Grilsgarter?' asked the Captain.

'Ah, that I don't know. Not even I can penetrate that secret. He keeps himself hidden, that one. But that tells us one thing: he is powerful and he is rich. Not many could stop their stories reaching my ears. I help pass his letters on, that's all, for a fee of course. Every few months a letter would be left in a particular spot. One of my men would take it and pass it on, that's all.'

'You've never tried to see who drops the letters?' asked Hephaestus.

'Oh yes, and a merry dance it led me too! Nothing came of it. This Grilsgarter knows how to hide himself. He could live a thousand miles away or he could be next door.'

'And the machine that took Mandrake?'

'I know nothing about that,' said the Painted Man. 'I heard it caused quite a stir though.'

'So this Grilsgarter wants the HELOTs and he kidnapped father for them,' said Hephaestus.

'Perhaps,' said the Painted Man. 'But he has never come to me asking for any.'

'We have to stop him,' said Hephaestus. He got up quickly.

'Wait,' said the Captain. 'Where are yer goin'?'

'I–' Hephaestus suddenly realised the Painted Man had not told them anything that would help them actually find Grilsgarter.

The Captain looked at the Painted Man. 'I want more than that. You've not told us enough.'

'Of course! Would I cheat you like that, my Captain?' said the Painted Man. He rubbed his hands together. 'There is more, but perhaps you don't want to hear it...'

'Get on with it.'

The Painted Man clapped his hands together excitedly. 'This Grilsgarter was careful. When he was looking for a ship and crew he knew how to go about it. He paid well to make sure he got the best and the most discreet. Oh, you'll love this, Captain, you really will. Guess whose ship our mysterious Grilsgarter chartered? It's delicious, it really is!'

'No,' replied the Captain. 'She didn't...'

'Aha! You've got it!'

The Captain stood up and strode out of the room.'

Of all the stupid things...' Hephaestus heard him mutter as he left. He was furious.

'Who are you talking about?' asked Hephaestus, thoroughly lost.

'His wife!' cried the Painted Man, laughing and clapping madly. He could barely keep himself in his chair. 'His very own, dear, sweet wife! Oh, this is priceless! Rapturous! Delightful! Divine! His very own wife!'

Hephaestus left the Painted Man cackling in his room and ran after the Captain. In the bar below, Hephaestus caught up with him.

'What do we do now?' he asked.

'Rosiet lives somewhere here in Guly Porta,' the Captain replied, looking straight ahead and not meeting Hephaestus' eye. 'We'll ask outside. Someone must know her.'

'This Rosiet is your wife?'

'Used to be,' said the Captain. 'A long time ago. We've not seen each other in a while.'

Hephaestus was just about to ask more but was stopped by the sound of a cry.

'Did you hear that?' he asked the Captain. 'Strange, I could have sworn that was Lud–'

Chapter Twelve:
Eleni

As soon as Ludwig heard the voice in the alley he cried out and bolted as fast as he could. It had been so close he had felt breath on his ear. He ran, heading for the street in front of him. But when he got to the end of the alley an arm shot out, knocking him to the ground. He scrambled in the dirt and looked up. Standing over him were a boy and girl of maybe sixteen or seventeen. The girl had a long blade pointing right at Ludwig's heart and the boy had a wicked smile on his face. Ludwig couldn't help but notice, despite his terror, that she had swirling patterns across her face just like the Captain had.

'What's this, Desses?' the girl asked the boy next to her. 'It looks like we've caught ourselves a snooper.' She knelt down, pressing the point of her weapon on Ludwig's chest and making him yelp. 'We don't like snoopers, do we Desses? Who sent you? Was it Russ? No, I bet it was Stevie. Stevie should've told you what happened to the last snooper of his we caught. He *wished* the slavers got him.'

'I'm no spy,' mumbled Ludwig. 'And I don't know any Russ or Stevie. I'm, I'm...' He racked his brains but couldn't think of a single excuse. This wasn't looking good.

'You were just pokin' around it the alley for fun were yer?' said the girl. She pressed on the blade again and Ludwig cried out in pain.

Then Ludwig heard someone call his name.

'LUDWIG?!'

The girl and boy turned and Ludwig looked between

them. There, standing in the door to *The Jester's Revenge* was Hephaestus and the Captain.

In a state of shock, Hephaestus caught sight of his brother and ran towards him, knocking aside the girl and boy who were standing over Ludwig. 'What are you *doing* here?!' he roared.

'Well–' started Ludwig. 'I... er...' He smiled sheepishly and almost laughed. Okay, he'd been found out, but at least the blade wasn't in his chest any more and the Captain and Hephaestus were here. That was something.

'Hey, you leave him alone!' said the girl quickly, picking both herself and her weapon up off the ground. 'He's ours. We caught him.'

Hephaestus turned and looked at the pair. He pulled up his cloak and uncovered his huge hands, balling them each into a fist.

'Touch him and I'll tear you apart.'

The girl smiled and the boy drew a knife from his belt. She looked Hephaestus over.

'Big 'un ain't yer? This'll be *fun.*'

The girl's blade moved so fast Ludwig could barely see it, but thankfully Hephaestus did. He jumped out of the way and quickly spun around as the boy called Desses hurled his knife. It missed Hephaestus only by an inch or so before clattering against a wall and falling to the ground. Ludwig thought about reaching for it, but with a weapon in his hand the chances of getting killed were even higher, especially as the only time he'd used a knife was in the kitchen. A fish he could gut; a person who's trying to kill him might be more tricky.

Hephaestus crouched and then launched himself at the boy and girl. They both stepped out of the way and took positions on each side of him, slowly sidestepping; the girl with her sabre and the boy with a new knife in his hand.

Ludwig could see they were toying with his brother.

Hephaestus was strong but he had no chance against these two.

Behind him, Ludwig heard footsteps. He looked round and saw more children appear out of the alley. Each one had a knife, sword or club in their hand too.

'Hephaestus...' Ludwig called quietly, not taking his eyes of the other children. 'I think we've got a problem.'

Then something very odd happened.

'Eleni,' came the Captain's voice, clear as a bell. 'Put down that sword *right now*, young lady.'

The girl looked round and the Captain walked up to her. 'I still recognise those marks,' he said pointing at her face. 'Since I put 'em there I should do!'

'How-?' She stopped and peered closely at the Captain. *'Dad?!'*

Chapter Thirteen:
A Surprising Past

'What did she say?' hissed Ludwig warily.

Hephaestus edged closed to his brother. 'I think she said-'

'She's my daughter, mate,' interrupted the Captain, putting a hand on the stunned girl's shoulder. 'Eleni, meet Ludwig and Hephaestus. Hephaestus is the one who was tryin' to crush yer skull like a grape. Ludwig is the one you were bullyin'.'

Eleni looked at the Captain. He was wearing his cloak again but the hood had slipped down a bit.

'Dad? Is... is that *really* you?' she asked. 'What's wrong...?' She reached out and pulled the hood down some more. The Captain's new face glinted in the moonlight. 'What happened to you?' She backed away at first, then seeing there was nothing to be afraid of, reached up again and touched her father's metal cheek. 'Why are you wearing this mask?'

'Eleni,' began the Captain. 'It's not a mask, love.'

Eleni listened stunned as the Captain told his daughter about Jack killing him all those months ago and Hephaestus giving him a new body.

'You're... *dead?'* Eleni managed once he had finished.

'No, not quite. I'm still alive up 'ere.' The Captain tapped the side of his head. 'It's still me, love. I'm just a bit different now, that's all.'

'You all right, Eleni?' said the boy called Desses. 'We can still cut 'em up if you like.'

Behind him yet more boys and girls were sliding out of the shadows.

Eleni shot out a hand. 'No. I... You should go. I'll call if

I need you.'

Desses looked back at the other children and shook his head. The gang looked at Ludwig, the Captain, and Hephaestus suspiciously then melted back into the alleyways around *The Jester's Revenge*. Ludwig couldn't see them any more, but he was sure they were still there, watching.

'Sorry to dump this on you, love,' said the Captain. 'I know it must be a bit of a shock.'

'*A bit!?*'

'You look like you're keepin' well anyway.'

Eleni looked murderously at the Captain.

'Well enough without *you,*' she snarled. Ludwig couldn't help but notice she had recovered from the shock of finding out about her father quite quickly. He supposed when you know someone well enough, their face stops mattering any more. Metal or flesh, it was still the same person after all. But she didn't seem too glad to see him, that much was obvious.

'And who were yer friends?' asked the Captain.

'My gang, dad. *They've* been my family since you left.'

Ludwig could see the Captain was picking his words carefully. 'Eleni,' said the Captain slowly, 'Yer shouldn't be doin' that sort of thing.'

Eleni looked at her father incredulously. 'What right have you got to say *that*? After all this time!'

'Love-'

'Don't you "love" me! What are you doing here, dad? I can't *believe* you had the nerve to come back!'

'I never intended to, but something has happened. I need t' see yer mum,' said the Captain. 'It's important. Can yer take me to 'er?'

'You can't order me about,' Eleni snapped.

'I'm not orderin', love. I'm askin'. Please. Take me to her.'

Eleni looked at her father strangely. 'What do you want with her after so long?' she asked. 'It's been ten *years.*'

'I think she's got wrapped up in somethin' she shouldn't. Has she said anythin' about a new job? It probably pays well too.'

'I... I don't see her much,' said Eleni, her voice now softer. 'But I heard she got back to port a few days ago and was doing a bit of celebrating.'

'She always did like that.'

'You know mum,' said Eleni quietly.

'Aye, that I do. Where is she?'

Eleni looked at the ground. 'I think she's livin' in the Uyllet district.'

'You don't know?'

'*You* don't know what it's been like since you left, dad. She got worse... with the drinking. I don't see her much any more. I can't.'

Ludwig felt suddenly uncomfortable. He knew he was seeing something very personal between the Captain and his daughter and he wished he wasn't.

'When did you leave?' asked the Captain.

'When I was eight or nine.'

'Eleni...' said the Captain.

'I know.'

'But she's your mum...'

'And she's *your* wife. What's your excuse?'

'You know my excuse,' said the Captain.

They were quiet for a time, then Eleni spoke up: 'Do you remember the way?' she asked.

'Maybe, but why don't yer show me anyway. Come on. I'd like to speak with you.'

Eleni looked like she was about to argue but instead turned and started walking. 'This way!' she called over her shoulder.

Meanwhile, Hephaestus picked Ludwig up off the ground and brushed him down.

'It looks like it's not just our family that's a mess,' he said, attempting a smile.

Unfortunately for the brothers, Eleni heard this. She spun round and Ludwig winced.

'What did you say?!' she screeched, running up to the brothers with her sword drawn again. She pointed it at Hephaestus.

'Sorry, I meant nothing by it,' replied Hephaestus, holding his hands up. 'It's just-'

'You had better not,' hissed Eleni, quieter now but still furious. She looked at the Captain and started walking away again. 'Well?' she snorted. 'Are you coming?'

'Yes, love,' the Captain replied, sounding weary. 'Lead the way.'

As they walked, Ludwig watched the Captain. He had never seen the Captain like this. He sounded strange; unsure of himself. He knew the Captain had done things before he had met him, but the idea of the Captain having a family of his own seemed very odd to Ludwig. And Ludwig even felt himself becoming jealous of this new girl.

'So you're in a gang,' said the Captain when they were a short distance away from *The Jester's Revenge*.

'Stop it, dad!' said Eleni, her voice making a few people still about at this hour quicken their step and their hands twitch in their cloaks nervously. *'You* left remember? I was *six* when you sailed off.'

'I know,' the Captain replied. 'I– I should have come back sooner. But it were hard and the longer I was away the harder it got. Then things changed in Pallenway. What happened between you and your mother? Tell me.'

'Mum tried to take care of me but... it was too much for her. She's not a bad person, but you broke her, do you know that?'

'I didn't have any choice, love. I had to go.'

'So she said.' Eleni huffed, then she caught sight of Ludwig looking at her. 'Finding this interesting?' she said coldly.

Ludwig shook his head and Eleni strode off, walking a little distance from the rest of them. The Captain glanced at Ludwig apologetically and then went to catch her up. They carried on talking in quieter voices.

The two brothers caught each other's eye. Both were as uncomfortable as the other.

'So you're here?' said Hephaestus.

'Yes,' said Ludwig quietly.

'You know the Captain is going to blow his top once this is sorted don't you?'

'Yes,' said Ludwig, now a whisper.

'It's good to see you though.'

Ludwig looked up at his brother and smiled. 'You too.'

Chapter Fourteen: Reunion

The Painted Man watched his recently departed guests walk down the street from the comfort of his room. 'Curious and more curious,' he said to himself as they disappeared. Then behind him, there was a small knock.

'Enter,' said the Painted Man, calling out absently while playing with the metal cube in his hands.

The door creaked and someone entered the room.

'I've come to report, sir.'

'My little bird,' said the Painted Man. 'Go, warm yourself by the fire. What have you to tell me, hmm?'

The newcomer walked across the room.

'Do yer want t' know who made the 'ELOTs?'

'I thought we already knew that, my boy. Mandrake von Guggenstein is their maker. A very sought after person right now too it seems.' *Perhaps too sought after*, thought the Painted Man. He didn't want to admit it, even to himself, but this Grilsgarter had scared him. He hadn't revealed everything when he told the Captain and Hephaestus about his attempts to track down the elusive Grilsgarter. The main reason the Painted Man had not been able to find him was because every man, woman and child he had sent to find Grilsgarter turned up dead. The very last one had been left in the Painted Man's own bed with a note attached.

DO NOT TRY THIS AGAIN.

- G.

The Painted Man shuddered at the memory as he came back to the present.

'What was that?' he asked. His guest had said something.

'I said: *not so,* sir,' said the newcomer.

The Painted Man's eyes narrowed.

'Go on.'

'It weren't Mandrake, it were the giant called 'Ephaestus. I over'eard the Captain talkin' to 'im.'

'And what did he say, pray?'

'He tol' the big one not t' *regret* buildin' 'em.'

The Painted Man held the cube up to his eye and smiled. 'Ah, now that is interesting and could prove useful to know. Well done, Senka.'

'No problem, sir,' said Senka.

The Painted Man crossed the room to a small desk set into one corner. He opened a drawer, took out a piece of paper and a pen and wrote something, then he handed the letter to Senka. 'Once the Mandrake situation has been put to bed one way or another, please pass this on. I trust you will use your discretion.'

Senka took the letter, read the front, and nodded. 'Yes sir. Of course, sir.'

The Painted Man returned to the window. 'By the way, I assume you were aware Ludwig von Guggenstein was on the *Kamaria* with you, yes?'

Senka's mouth dropped open. '*No!* No one said he were on board, I swear!'

'Not to worry. It looks like the Captain didn't know himself. I imagine he sneaked aboard.'

'Sneaked?'

The Painted Man pointed and Senka came up next to him. Senka looked out of the window.

'Lian!'

'Who?'

'That's the lad we picked up just before we left Beacon. He looked as lost as a little lamb an' I thought he were an orphan from the Terror. That's *the* Ludwig!'

'You know him then? Good.'

'What d'yer want me t' do now?' Senka asked.

'Go back to the *Kamaria*. Deliver the note when the time is right and keep your eyes and ears open. Send word when you get chance. If Mandrake dies or is already dead, Hephaestus von Guggenstein could be the most important person in the world.'

'Yes, sir,' said Senka. The door creaked again and he left.

'Good boy,' said the Painted Man.

The Painted Man went to one of the soft chairs and let himself rest. He had carved out a life for himself by knowing how to pick his battles and who not to annoy. Right now, while he was well aware that Mandrake von Guggenstein would have no end of buyers, he would be stirring up a hornets' nest if he did catch him. Grilsgarter would come after him for one. No, the Painted Man would have to play the long game. But what would be the next move?

'Hephaestus...' he muttered to himself.

There was another knock on his door, much heavier and louder than the first.

'What is it?' said the Painted Man annoyed at being brought out of his thoughts.

The man who had entered stared at the floor. 'We've found him, sir.'

The Painted Man's eyes lit up. *Aha!* 'Today just gets better and better,' he said standing up. He thought for a while and then said: 'This is what I want you to do...'

Chapter Fifteen: Rosiet

Soon enough, and with only few people attempting to attack them on their journey, Ludwig, Hephaestus, the Captain, and Eleni came to a small house on a quiet street on the outskirts of Guly Porta. A dim light shone in the windows.

'She's in,' said Eleni.

The Captain walked over to the front door and knocked. They waited but there was no answer. He pushed the door and to his surprise, it opened. The Captain went first. 'Rosiet?' he called out. 'Are you there?'

'Mum?' said Eleni, going in after him. 'It's just me.'

Ludwig and Hephaestus followed.

The hallway of the house was dark and grubby. A battered picture hung at an angle on a stained wall and on the floor mud had been traipsed in and left to dry. It looked like the place hadn't been cleaned for some time.

'She doesn't use her house much,' said Eleni, looking slightly embarrassed. 'Her ship's much better. She spends most of her time on that.'

'You should see our old home,' said Ludwig, remembering the empty, now burnt down castle. He popped his head through the door of the closest room. It was much like the hall. 'Pretty similar anyway.'

'Eleni,' came the voice of the Captain from another room. 'You'd best come here, love.'

Eleni went to her father. Ludwig and Hephaestus followed.

At the back of the house, Ludwig found the Captain standing in a bedroom. It was even worse than the hall and the other rooms Ludwig had seen. Clothes were thrown everywhere and in between lay empty bottles with flies buzzing around their tops. Pushed up against the far wall was a bed, and on the bed was a woman. She wasn't moving.

'Mum?' said Eleni, rushing over. She knelt down and took one of the woman's hands. 'Mum, it's me, it's Eleni. I'm here. Wake up. Dad's here too. He– he needs to talk to you.'

The woman on the bed didn't move.

Eleni shook her mother's hand and then rocked her shoulder. 'Mum, please, wake up...'

The Captain walked over to his daughter.

'Eleni...'

'But... *no!* Mum, come on. Wake up!' Desperation was in her voice and Ludwig's heart sank. 'Please... please...'

'Love, I'm sorry,' said the Captain.

'No!'

'She's gone.'

'She can't be dead! There's no reason!' Eleni grabbed her mother's shoulders and shook hard, then she slumped against the bed, buried her head in her arms, and started sobbing. The Captain stood over her, saying nothing.

Ludwig and Hephaestus, feeling like they shouldn't be there, walked outside leaving the grieving family in peace.

Chapter Sixteen:
A Plan of Revenge

'Did you know he had a family?' asked Ludwig, wanting to break the uncomfortable silence as he and Hephaestus sat on the step of Rosiet's house. It had been months since Ludwig had spoken to his brother and right now he wanted to do so more than ever.

Hephaestus shook his head. 'No, it's news to me. I didn't see him as a family man somehow.'

'We should ask him about his old life sometime,' said Ludwig.

'I doubt he'll tell us anything.'

'No, maybe not.'

Hephaestus looked at his brother hard. 'Ludwig, what are you *doing* here?'

Ludwig shrugged. 'I didn't want to be left behind,' he explained. He told Hephaestus how he got on board the ship and what he had been doing on the voyage.

Hephaestus snorted. 'That's it? You felt *left out?*'

'And... I know it sounds stupid but I feel like father is my responsibility because of what happened. I could have killed him, Hephaestus. I could have stopped all of this happening. Instead, he's wandering about free.' Ludwig glanced back at the house. 'And I guess it looks like he's hurting people again.'

Hephaestus looked at his brother. 'Ludwig, you don't know! Father didn't escape, he was kidnapped! He *couldn't* have done this! It looks like it was this Grilsgarter, or at least someone who worked for him. He took father and wants him for something. I think it's so he can build more HELOTs.'

'Kidnapped?'

'Yes!'

'But...'

'He's not your responsibility in *any* way,' said Hephaestus. 'Don't think otherwise. Look, I'll talk to the Captain. He'll probably need a bit of time after what's going on—' he looked back at Rosiet's house. 'I'll explain this to him later. I'd stay out of his way for a while though.'

Ludwig suddenly realised what his brother had said. '*HELOTs?* Not again!'

'Maybe.'

Ludwig slumped on the kerb. 'So what's the plan?'

'I don't know. We know the Captain's wife was the one sailing the ship Grilsgarter and father left Beacon on. Now she's dead we may not have any more clues. Perhaps we can ask around, see if anyone else knows anything or saw something. Maybe one of her crew could help.'

Ludwig nodded but had a horrible feeling if the captain of the ship that had taken Grilsgarter was dead, the crew weren't likely to be around either.

'Well—' he began, but saw that something else had caught Hephaestus' attention. He followed his brother's gaze and saw a young, skinny boy of perhaps eight years old or so walking towards them.

'You wiv someone called "the Captain"?' the boy squeaked when he was nearer.

'We might be,' said Hephaestus. 'Why?'

'Yer got t' come wiv me.'

'Really?' said Hephaestus. 'And why is that?'

'Painted Man sent me,' said the boy. 'The man you want, Guggenstone. He's outside town right now. Some people are takin' 'im away. You gotta come quick though. They'll be goin' soon.'

Hephaestus didn't hesitate.

'Captain!' he called out.

The Captain appeared outside Rosiet's house with his daughter beside him. Eleni had her head bent low and kept her face hidden from the brothers. The Captain had an arm around her shoulder.

'What is it, Hephaestus?' asked the Captain.

Hephaestus told the Captain what the boy had said.

'The man you're here for?' Eleni snarled. She looked up. 'Did he do this to mum?'

'I don't think so, love,' replied the Captain. 'But he does have somethin' to do with it.' He looked at the boy. 'Where are they?'

'Painted Man says they're at the Fallen Arches outside o' town. I'm meant t' take yer there.'

'We need to go back to the ship first,' said the Captain. 'I need my crew.' He looked at Ludwig, Hephaestus and Eleni. 'And I'm not havin' any of you put in danger. You can stay with the ship and I'm in no mood to argue,' Then he noticed the boy tugging on his sleeve.

'Yer need t' come now!' said the boy. 'No time to go back to yer ship. Come on! They've got a boat and they'll be sailin' soon.'

'But-'

'Listen to him, dad. I'm coming,' said Eleni.

'Love,' said the Captain. He knelt down and took hold of his daughter. 'I'll find whoever did this, I swear. I'll tear 'em apart. But you shouldn't get involved.'

'Don't talk to me like that,' said Eleni. 'You need people? I can *help.*' She put her fingers in her mouth and whistled. Then she quickly wiped he sleeve across her eyes to get rid of the tears that remained.

Out of the darkness on the side of Rosiet's house, the boy called Desses appeared. He scowled at Ludwig and Hephaestus as he walked over to Eleni. 'What's up, El?'

he asked.

'Get the gang. We've got work to do.'

'Eleni, don't you dare do what I think yer doin',' said the Captain.

'They killed her, dad. They came to her house and killed her. They've got to pay for that.' She looked at Desses. 'Meet us at the copse near the Fallen Arches. Bring everyone.'

Desses nodded and slipped back into the night. Ludwig didn't hear a single footstep.

'Eleni...' began the Captain, but she ignored him and started striding off.

'I'm going to kill them, dad,' said Eleni coldly. 'You can come if you want.'

'You're your mother's daughter all right,' murmured the Captain. He turned to Ludwig and Hephaestus, who had been standing silent the whole time. 'You two, come with me and do exactly what I say, got it?'

Hephaestus and Ludwig nodded quickly.

'Good. Let's get this over with.' The Captain started off after his daughter. The brothers followed behind.

'Glad you came along?' asked Hephaestus.

Ludwig shook his head.

Chapter Seventeen:
The Fallen Arches

The Fallen Arches stood a mile or so outside of Guly Porta on the bank of the river Olpe. The arches themselves were all that was left of an ancient temple built in a time long before the Great Migration and the founding of Guly Porta. They were twisted and strange, and would cast uncomfortable shadows that seemed to writhe on the ground. Few people from Guly Porta would visit them, even before they had heard the stories about those who had gone to the arches and vanished mysteriously. Ludwig, who had not heard the stories or the rumours, still shivered when he saw them. It was as if a cold wind blew from the very stones.

'The Painted Man sez he'll see yer soon,' said the boy, looking at the Captain. He ran back to town leaving everyone else in the shadows of some tall trees that stood near the Arches. Ludwig wondered what he meant but didn't ask.

Right now it was still night time but he could just make out the others in the moonlight. Above, clouds were gathering.

'What now, love?' The Captain whispered.

'Wait,' said Eleni. She put her hands to her mouth and made a noise like a bird-call. Moments later there was a rustle nearby and Desses appeared again.

'What did you see?' asked Eleni, all business now; her tears gone.

'There's about twenty of 'em,' Desses reported. 'With rifles and pistols. Slavers by the look of it.'

'Slavers?' said the Captain.

Desses shot a look at Eleni. 'It's okay, you can tell him,' she said.

'They've been sniffin' around Guly Porta a lot recently. The governor don't mind as long as they don't take anyone important, so it's the gangs 'ave lost the most people to 'em. Jaymes' gang were taken a few months ago, including even Jaymes hisself. Whoever's in charge never shows his face and if we kill any, the only thing that happens is more come down the river and more are taken.'

'Slavers...' muttered the Captain. Ludwig could see the Captain was angry. Even though his face never changed the Captain now had a way of moving that showed his emotions just as well. 'I've had my fill of slavers for a lifetime.'

'Anything else goin' on out there?' asked Eleni.

'Only that their boat's pointing up river, not down,' Desses replied.

'That's strange,' said Eleni.

'Why's that?' asked Ludwig.

'They should be going out to sea, not up river. There's no point. The Ople doesn't go anywhere. There's a few villas dotted about and if you go far enough, you can get to Hulin Porta in a day cross country, but that's it. It's just villages, farmland, and a few estates; it's lots of nothing that way.

'It must have something to do with Mandrake and Grilsgarter then,' said the Captain.

'There's slaves with 'em as well,' said Desses. 'I recognised a few faces from the other gangs.'

Ludwig saw Eleni's face. She looked sick. Then Ludwig realised he had his own reasons for being horrified. *These slaves were for Mandrake and Grilsgarter...*

'How many of us are there?' asked Eleni.

'Everyone's here barrin' Taddler and Yincy. They got caught thievin' early t'day. I thought they were in the lock-up but it looks like the governor sold 'em off straight away. They're with the slaves.'

Ludwig saw Eleni's fist tighten. 'That'll have to do.'

Suddenly the sky rumbled. Rain began to fall.

'It was clear a moment ago!' hissed Ludwig, crouching closer to the trees to avoid the weather.

'We're in the tropics,' said the Captain. 'The weather is changeable here.' He took off his cape and passed it to Ludwig. 'I doubt I'll be needin' it for a while and I don't feel the cold any more.'

Ludwig threw the cloak over him but didn't pull it tight. The night was still hot despite the wet. He listened to the water pattering above and tried to stop himself feeling nervous.

'Eleni, I'm not happy about this,' said the Captain. 'Your gang are jus' kids.'

'Kids that have been livin' on the streets of Guly Porta most of their lives, dad,' replied Eleni. 'They know how to stay alive.'

The Captain rolled up his sleeves and his mechanical arms glistened in the rain. He wasn't in his other body which was twice as big and much stronger, but this one was still good enough.

'Ludwig, Hephaestus,' he called to the brothers, 'you two stay here.'

Ludwig, knowing better than to argue right now, nodded. Then Hephaestus said what Ludwig had been thinking.

'The Slaves...' said Hephaestus. 'Captain, you know what they might be for...'

'I know, mate,' said the Captain. He looked at his daughter. 'You seem to be in charge. What shall we do?'

'Come with me,' she said.

Ludwig and Hephaestus watched as the Captain, his daughter, and Desses disappeared into the night. When they had gone, he crept forward and peeked through the leaves. Beyond, a few hundred feet away or more, a group of men stood milling about near a wooden jetty that went out a short way into the river. They held lanterns in one hand and rifles in the other. At the end of the jetty was a boat and the slaves were being led on to it.

Ludwig looked closely and his eyes widened. *'There he is!'* he hissed. *'I can see him!'* Hephaestus came up behind him and Ludwig pointed to a figure standing near the other men. It was their father.

'So he *was* kidnapped,' said Hephaestus.

A tall man turned up his collar with one hand as the rain fell. He held his rifle tightly in the other and thought to himself: I'm not happy right now. He'd served the Grilsgarters for seven years but he certainly hadn't signed up for this. Slaves? It wasn't right, no matter what. But it wasn't like he had a choice in the matter.

He looked to his left. The slaves were loading the boat. The tall man whose name was Bobby had done some awful things in his life, he'd admit that, but slaving made his stomach turn. He stood a little away from them and kept his eyes from catching the hopeless, despairing looks on the slaves' faces. He looked past the slaves and spotted his colleague Ekhert on the boat vanishing below deck. Bobby wondered if Ekhert hated this as much as he did.

'When are we goin'?' said Bobby to the nearest slaver.

'Soon,' grunted the slaver, a disgusting, scabrous man that stunk of old sweat. 'They've nearly loaded everythin' on board.'

Bobby looked back and into the darkness beyond the lantern light. The Fallen Arches were briefly silhouetted against the sky before the storm blocked out the moon and stars. He shivered. This place was giving him the creeps and he was hating every minute of it.

Ssshum!

Bobby jumped. The slaver he'd just spoken to let out a gurgled cry and fell to the floor.

'What the–?' he started but he didn't get chance to finish his sentence. Suddenly the bushes all around him were alive with cat-cries and bird screeches. Terrified, he pulled up his shaking rifle and fired. There were more screams as more slavers fell. A thump behind him made him jump. Bobby spun around and saw another man dead on the floor. Standing over him was a young girl smiling evilly.

Eleni flew at Bobby, her sabre swinging as she went. He put up his rifle just in time and her blade caught on it.

Bobby grinned madly.

'I don't want to hurt yer, missy,' he said. 'But I will if I 'ave to.'

Eleni snarled and ran at him. 'Who killed her?' she screamed, bringing her blade down.

Bobby dived out of the way, but his feet went from under him and he rolled across the ground.

'What yer on about?' he shouted back.

'My mum! Rosiet!'

Rosiet, thought Bobby. The woman who owned the ship Grilsgarter used to bring Mandrake here. But she had known too much and Grilsgarter didn't want any loose ends...

Bobby glanced towards Ekhert and Eleni followed his gaze.

The man on the boat, thought Eleni. The look Bobby had given had been enough. That man on the boat had killed her mother.

Eleni circled as Bobby got up. She looked to her right and so did he. Desses' knife sliced through the air and Bobby crashed to the ground.

Bobby felt the life drain out of him, but he managed to pull himself up just a little and looked again towards the boat. Ekhert was on deck.

'Ekhert!' moaned Bobby, reaching out towards his friend, but when Ekhert saw him he shook his head. Ekhert then turned to cut the ropes attaching the boat to the jetty and the ship's engine roared.

'Don't leave...' muttered Bobby as he closed his eyes.

Once Eleni had finished him off, she looked up to see her mother's killer moving up river on the Slaver's boat. Some of Eleni's gang grabbed the rifles the slavers had dropped and started shooting, but they didn't stop the boat and their shots missed the man.

Eleni took a rifle, aimed, and fired. The bullet went wide and splinters flew up near the man's head, who then ducked down, out of sight.

'Blast it!' cried Eleni, throwing the rifle to the ground.

'Forget about him, love,' said the Captain appearing next to her. He looked at the slaves that had been left behind. 'We've got what we came for.'

Eleni watched the boat disappear into the storm. 'I didn't,' she said.

When the gunfire had stopped, Ludwig burst from his hiding place and ran towards the slaves left on the bank of the river. Hephaestus came up behind him; their feet slipping on the wet earth.

Near the jetty, Ludwig saw his father sitting on the floor with shackles around his wrists.

'Ludwig, have you come to rescue me?' asked his father, holding up the shackles so his son could see them clearly. 'Once again, I appear to be imprisoned.'

'No, he hasn't,' said the Captain before Ludwig could

reply. 'Get up, Mandrake.'

Ludwig's father stood up. 'Would *you* mind?' he said, offering his wrists to the Captain.

'Not yet.' The Captain went up to the other slaves that had been left behind and broke each one of their shackles in turn with his hands. The slaves looked at him in terror.

'Run,' said the Captain. 'Get away from here.' The slaves didn't have to be told twice. Most ran, but a couple of the younger slaves went to Eleni and Desses.

'Taddler, Yincy, what *happened?'* asked Eleni.

'We weren't doin' anything, we swear!' said one of the boys. 'The governor's men jus' took us off the street. Honest, El, there were no reason!'

Eleni nodded her head. 'All right, but you should stay away from the governor's men whether you've done something or not. Go to Desses, he'll tell you what to do.'

Meanwhile, the Captain walked up to Mandrake, picked him up, and threw him over one shoulder.

'What *are* you doing?' Mandrake cried out in surprise. 'This is rather degrading.'

'I don't care,' replied the Captain. He walked up to his daughter. 'Eleni, come with me. I want to talk to you before we leave. I've got a proposal for you.'

Desses took a step forward but Eleni stopped him. She looked at her friend. 'Wait, Desses. I'm going. I'll send word soon, don't worry.'

'Hephaestus,' said the Captain. 'Grab Ludwig.'

'What? *Hey!'* Ludwig cried as Hephaestus swept him up as if he weighed nothing. 'Hephaestus! Let go of me!'

'Quiet, Ludwig,' said the Captain. 'I'm in no mood, mate.'

Ludwig looked pleadingly at his brother.

'Sorry,' said Hephaestus. 'Captain's orders.'

Chapter Eighteen:
Interrogation

When they returned to the *Kamaria*, the Captain threw Mandrake into one cabin, locked it, then went to another and opened the door.

'Eleni, the galley is down there,' said the Captain. 'Go and get yourself something to eat and I'll come and find you later. I need to speak to Ludwig.'

Eleni nodded her head and walked away, but Ludwig couldn't help but notice the nasty smile she threw his way.

The Captain looked at Hephaestus. 'Bring him in here,' he said, opening another cabin door and stepped inside. Hephaestus followed with Ludwig still on his shoulder.

'You've got a *hell* of a lot of explainin' to do young man,' said the Captain after Ludwig had been dropped into a chair. Hephaestus stood to one side, letting the Captain speak. The Captain didn't shout, he didn't need to. 'Believe me, mate, I've got no patience for any games. What are you doin' 'ere?'

'I– I don't know,' said Ludwig quietly.

'Of course yer know!' said the Captain. 'Come on Ludwig, out with it. Do yer have *any* idea how angry I am, mate? And yer grandmother must being goin' spare with worry.'

'I wrote her a letter...' Ludwig replied.

'When?'

'At Okla.'

'Oh, well that's all right then,' said the Captain sarcastically. 'I'm sure she thinks you're perfectly well and has absolutely nothing to worry about.'

'I wanted to come with you!' Ludwig blurted out.

'That didn't give yer a right to!' the Captain shouted back.

He huffed. 'So... you've been hidin' on the ship?'

'Yes,' said Ludwig sullenly. He told the Captain what he had been doing on the voyage.

'Senka got you on board? I think I'll be havin' words with him too. Sneaky little devil.'

'It wasn't his fault! He thought he was helping me!'

'So you lied to him.'

'Well... yes. But–!' Ludwig knew he couldn't win. He'd made mistake upon mistake.

'Don't "but" me, mate. Of all the stupid, irresponsible things yer could 'ave done; of all the idiot things, I never thought you'd do this!' The Captain looked at Hephaestus. 'Did you know he was here?'

'No!' rumbled Hephaestus. 'It's a surprise to me too.' He glanced at Ludwig. 'Look, Captain, can I speak to you before you punish Ludwig?'

'All right,' said the Captain. Hephaestus took him to outside and Ludwig ran to the door to see if he could hear anything, but they were too quiet.

When they had finished, they came back in again and the Captain looked at Ludwig. 'After I've spoken to Mandrake,' the Captain began. 'We're goin' to 'ave a long conversation. But be thankful your brother's here. He's explained a few things and, well, I'm still not happy but maybe I can understand what yer did. Hephaestus, stay with Ludwig while I speak to your father.'

'Don't you want me there?' asked Hephaestus.

'No I don't think that would be a good idea,' the Captain replied.

Hephaestus grabbed the Captain's arm as he turned to leave. 'Don't... don't hurt him,' said Hephaestus.

The Captain looked at the brothers but said nothing, then he left the cabin. When he closed the door behind him, it nearly came off the hinges.

'Thanks,' said Ludwig.

'I told him what you told me,' said Hephaestus. 'But you need to be on your best behaviour from now on.'

'I know,' said Ludwig.

Outside Ludwig's cabin, the Captain saw Sir Notsworth. He was in the corridor chewing on a chicken leg.

'Hullo,' said Sir Notsworth. 'Any luck? It's been pretty quiet here–'

'I've got Mandrake,' said the Captain.

Sir Notsworth dropped his chicken leg. *What?*

The Captain pointed to the second cabin door. 'He's in there. Come with me. We need t' talk to him.' He quickly explained what had happened at the Fallen Arches.

'But... but *how?*' asked Sir Notsworth.

'We were tipped off.'

'You've only been gone an hour or so!'

'I know. We were lucky... I think. Oh, and Ludwig's here too,' continued the Captain.

'*Ludwig?*' spluttered Sir Notsworth. 'How on earth did he manage that?'

'He sneaked aboard at Beacon. I'm furious with 'im but I can't 'elp but be a little impressed. He's been livin' with the deckhands and workin' in the galley with Chef. I always seem to underestimate him. I should've learned when he went after his father the last time. He looks so meek, but he's one of the most bull-headed people I've ever met.'

Sir Notsworth laughed. 'Well I never. He gets that from his father, you know. Mandrake is just the same. So is Matilda. They're all pulling in their own directions. It's no wonder things break. Is there anything *else* I should know?' asked Sir Notsworth.

'And my daughter's on board.'

'You're joking, sir.'

'No, mate. I wish I were.'

'I think I need to sit down!' said Sir Notsworth, taking out a handkerchief and patting his brow with it. 'I knew this was going to be an eventful trip but this is too much! So... what's your plan now?'

'We'll speak to Mandrake,' replied the Captain. 'I want to know what's goin' on between him an' this Grilsgarter.'

'Right you are,' said Sir Notsworth and followed the Captain into Mandrake's cabin.

'My patience has gone mate,' the Captain growled at Mandrake. 'I want to know *exactly* what is goin' on and if yer start playing games I'm sailing out to the middle of the ocean and throwing you overboard, yer understand?'

The Captain looked at his prisoner. Mandrake sat on a plain wooden chair in an otherwise empty cabin. His clothes were torn and dirty and he looked like he hadn't eaten for some time. But that could wait, thought the Captain. He almost felt sorry for Mandrake.

Almost.

'Mandrake, have you told this Grilsgarter how to make the HELOTs?' said the Captain, grabbing Mandrake by the collar and lifting him up.

'I'm sorry,' said Mandrake quietly, his head turned away. 'I had too.'

'Mandrake,' said Sir Notsworth. 'How *could* you?'

The Captain let Mandrake go in disgust and he slumped back into the chair. Mandrake pulled up his shirt and they saw bruises across his chest; lots of them.

'Grilsgarter can be very persuasive,' said Mandrake.

'That's... awful' said Sir Notsworth. Where is Grilsgarter

now?'

'He ran home. He lives further up river. He left me with those men to take me to his villa.'

'Ran home?' said the Captain. 'You don't mean...'

'The machine *is* Aliester Grilsgarter. He was the one who took me from Beacon.'

Sir Notsworth whistled.

'Why didn't he just take yer himself?' asked the Captain, ignoring the revelation for the time being.

'Aliester doesn't have much patience and he's not gentle. If he had carried me all the way I wouldn't have survived, so he left me with his men and went on ahead. He had what he wanted anyway.'

'We have to stop him,' said the Captain. 'Who and *what* is he?'

'I cannot agree more.' Mandrake straightened his clothes and brushed off the dirt. 'Aliester is an old student of mine from a long time ago when I lived in Juleto,' he explained. 'I needed money and he wanted me as a teacher. I took him under my wing so to speak and he paid me handsomely.'

'And you turned him into *that?*'

'I most certainly did not! Well, at least not immediately. Aliester was a golden goose; I wanted him with me as much as possible. He comes from a very wealthy family and that wealth was going straight into my pocket.'

'What happened?' asked the Captain. 'I read his letter to you. He blames you for something.'

'Letter? Ah, you've been rooting around in my things haven't you?' Mandrake sighed. 'I suppose it doesn't matter now anyway.'

'Get on with it Mandrake,' said the Captain.

'Some time ago there was an attempt on my life. I've made quite a few enemies over the years doing what I do, and one such person was more persistent than the others. Someone died, someone else got upset, you know how it is. But the killer wasn't all that bright. He came to my laboratory and attacked Aliester instead of me. When I came home I found Aliester dying. Seeing my golden goose about to slip from my fingers, I decided to test out some new ideas I'd had recently. I thought it would be possible to keep someone alive after death through the use of certain scientific methods and principles. I had tried with animals and had some success, but never on a person.'

'The HELOTs,' said Sir Notsworth.

'Not quite,' Mandrake replied. 'Hephaestus can be credited with their invention.' Mandrake looked at the Captain. 'And I see Hephaestus has been continuing his work. *You* could think of Aliester as an ancestor of yours in some ways. He is essentially a prototype of the HELOTs, but unfortunately when I built him I didn't know how to keep his mind alive without his body the way Hephaestus did. Rather than the cubes Hephaestus created, I had discovered certain chemicals could be used to stop his mind and body dying completely. However, these chemicals are very hard to produce and therefore very expensive. I only did what I did to Aliester because of his family's wealth. Aliester has to use the chemicals at an astonishing rate, and while Aliester is a triumph if I do say so myself, few people could afford to live like that for longer than a couple of days.'

'Did you even *ask* him if he wanted to be changed?' asked Sir Notsworth. 'He doesn't seem too happy about what you've done.'

'No, alas Aliester is not happy,' Mandrake replied. 'I was a little... short-sighted when I decided to keep him alive. You see, because of his change, Aliester was caught in quite a bind. His family had very high hopes for him but his transformation has meant certain problems have arisen.'

'What problems? asked the Captain.

'He was being groomed by his family to become a ruler. However, his new form means no one would accept him.'

'What did you offer him?' asked the Captain.

Mandrake paused. 'I was going to give him an army.'

'The HELOTs,' said Sir Notsworth.

'Quite. They had actually been for Aliester originally, but when the first was created I saw what I could accomplish with them myself. I had my own... issues that I wanted to deal with and power is extremely attractive after all. Obviously Aliester was a little upset with this.'

The Captain turned to Sir Notsworth. 'At least we have some idea what we're dealing with.' He looked back at Mandrake. 'And do you know where Aliester lives?'

'Oh yes, his villa is a few days journey upriver,' replied Mandrake.

The Captain walked over to the cabin door, opened it, and let two of his crew in. He pointed at Mandrake. 'Take 'im below.'

The men nodded and each grabbed one of Mandrake's arms.

'Wait!' cried Mandrake as he was hoisted up. 'You haven't asked me the most important thing,'

'Yes,' said the Captain. 'Go on.'

'You don't know who Aliester's family are.'

'I don't care about some back-water king,' said the Captain.

'Ah, you haven't quite understood. Aliester's family had to change their name to 'Grilsgarter' years ago. Their old name used to be *Petraya.*'

'You can't be serious,' said Sir Notsworth.

'Oh, but I am.'

The Captain's fist smashed into the wall. Sir Notsworth was glad it wasn't the hull.

'Get 'im out of here,' said the Captain and the two crewmen

pulled at Mandrake, taking him out of the room.

'You know what this means, don't you?' said Sir Notsworth.

'Yes, mate,' replied the Captain. 'We've got a lot of work to do.'

While the Captain was talking to their father, Ludwig and Hephaestus sat in the cabin and waited. A short time later there was a knock on the cabin door and one of the crew asked Ludwig and Hephaestus to come on deck.

'What's going on?' asked Ludwig.

'Somethin' serious,' said the crewman.

When they got on deck, Ludwig found himself standing with everyone else from the *Kamaria*. Eleni appeared next to him with an apple in her hand while Hephaestus stood behind. Ludwig looked around and also saw Senka and Chef. Senka looked at him in wide-eyed surprise, while Chef caught Ludwig's eye and smiled cryptically. When he got a chance, Ludwig would have to explain things to them. It was another thing he wasn't looking forward to.

At the ship's stern, there was a commotion and Ludwig saw the Captain appear next to the ship's wheel.

'Listen!' the Captain called out. 'Settle down now, I've got news.'

The crew went quiet.

'We've got Mandrake–' he began, but he couldn't carry on over the crew's loud cheers.

'*WAIT!*' the Captain boomed. 'You ain't heard everythin'.'

The crew quietened again, surprised by how loud the Captain managed to make his voice.

'Look, I'll be honest with yer. It's like this. You remember the 'ELOTs right?'

The crew was silent. A few muttered prayers. They

remembered.

'... Well, there's a risk someone else might be makin' 'em.'

The crew gasped and started murmuring to one another.

'Settle down!' shouted the Captain. 'Look, if we're fast enough, we can stop 'em!'

The murmuring quietened and the crew looked more confident.

'I'm guessin' they aren't being built just yet. If we can get to where we're goin' in time then we can stop this before it gets out of control.'

The crew looked happier.

'There's another thing,' the Captain continued. 'The man who grabbed von Guggenstein... well, he's a Petraya.'

Some of the crew whistled while other just looked at the Captain in disbelief.

'I know what yer thinkin' mates because I thought the same. But he'll need time t' make the HELOTs and I say we stop 'im before he has a chance. I want this ship ready to sail in the next few hours. We know this Grilsgarter is up there.' The Captain pointed to the mouth of the river Ople. 'So off you go and prepare. I want any supplies bought over from Guly Porta and everything ready for river travel. Quick now, hop to it!'

The crew scattered and started preparing to set sail. The Captain came over to where Ludwig was standing.

'Right,' began the Captain. 'First things first. Eleni, my proposal: I want you t' come with us, love.'

'I'm coming,' she replied without even hesitating.

'I want yer here with me but I know-' The Captain then realised what his daughter had said. 'But what about your gang?'

'I don't want to leave them,' said Eleni. 'But I saw who killed mum. He's gone up river and that's where I want to be. The gang'll have to survive on their own for a bit.'

'No, love,' said the Captain. 'That's not what I meant. I want you here from now on. No goin' back to Guly Porta.'

Eleni was shocked. 'Dad... I don't think so... my gang... I have to look after them.'

The Captain looked hard at her.

'They ever thought about sailin'?' he asked.

'You want them to join your *crew?*'

'It'd be a better life than the one they've got now,' said the Captain. 'They'll get paid, they'll get fed. I'm not offerin' much, but they're welcome to join us. I saw what they're like. Nothin' but skin an' bones.'

'I– I need t' talk to them.'

'Good. Yer've got two hours. Take a boat to shore,' said the Captain. 'Find yer gang and tell 'em what I said. They're welcome to join us but they ain't got much time to decide.'

Eleni nodded and ran off towards the longboats.

The Captain turned to Ludwig. 'And as for you mate, you're to stay 'ere. I'm still mad, but yer here now an' there's nothin' much I can do about it. I've spoken to Chef and he's said yer've been a god-send so you can continue workin' in the galley, but if I hear any complaints from anyone...'

Ludwig nodded quickly. 'Yes, Captain. Sorry, Captain.'

'Good.' The Captain turned and was about to leave when Ludwig spoke up.

'Captain? What's a "Petraya"?' asked Ludwig

'Didn't yer dad teach you history?' said the Captain turning back round. 'Well here's a quick lesson. The last Petraya was called Nikolis. You know the square in Beacon? It's named after him. He called himself Superbus Excelsior as his family ruled an empire that covered Pallenway and Galleesha, plus quite a few other countries, hundreds of years ago. He was a cruel man, Ludwig. Stories about him and his kin would make your blood run cold.'

'What happened to them?'

'About two hundred years ago there was an uprisin'. It were a terrible war and thousands of lives were lost, but eventually those who fought against Nikolis won. They stormed his palace in Beacon, the very same one you were in for yer father's execution, and dragged him and 'is family into the square where they were executed. After that, the countries of the old empire were swept clean of the Petraya family. You hear rumours now and then of a descendent springin' up and tryin' to claim the throne again, but most of them are just madmen or con artists. Problem is I don't doubt for a minute we've found a real one this time.'

'But does it change anything?' asked Ludwig.

'A lot, mate,' the Captain replied. 'Anyone havin' the HELOTs is dangerous, but at least everyone can rally round and fight back when it's some unknown like yer father tryin' to take over. A Petraya is different.'

'Why?'

'Because quite a lot of people think the rule of the Superbus Excelsiors was a golden age. They forget the blood and the death and just remember the splendour. They'll even be able to ignore the fact that this new Petraya is almost all machine. There are a lot of people, like those you saw in the audience chamber when your father was goin' to be executed, that may even support him. And with the HELOTs as well it'd be impossible to get rid of the Petrayas again and from what yer father has said, it looks like this Grilsgarter wants his family's empire back. We've got to stop 'im before any of this starts.'

Ludwig nodded but said nothing. It all seemed too much.

'Go below,' said the Captain. 'And make yourself useful.' The Captain looked at Ludwig's brother. 'Hephaestus, come with me.'

Chapter Nineteen:
The Ople

That evening, Hephaestus came up onto the deck and looked up. It was a clear night and the stars shone brightly as the *Kamaria* sailed down the river Ople. He had come from the galley and was carrying a plate of food in his hand. He looked around and saw Eleni sitting at the prow with her legs dangling over the side. He went over, setting the plate down nearby.

'What's this?' she asked, seeing the plate.

'Dinner,' Hephaestus replied.

'Oh... Thanks.'

'Where's your gang?' Hephaestus asked. He hadn't seen any new faces wandering around the ship.

Eleni shifted uncomfortably. 'Most of them stayed,' she said quietly. 'They didn't like the idea of leaving Guly Porta. I don't blame them either.'

'Most?'

There was a cough and Hephaestus turned. Desses appeared and sat down next to Eleni. Hephaestus then saw Desses slip a hand into Eleni's. *Ah,* thought Hephaestus. *It's like that.*

'Desses came and a couple of others as well,' said Eleni. 'But that's it.'

'I'm sorry to hear that,' said Hephaestus.

'It doesn't matter. Maybe it's time to move on anyway. I don't think I want to stay in that town any more, not after seeing mum...' Eleni trailed off.

'I understand.'

Eleni turned and looked hard at Hephaestus. 'I've got to

ask, what happened to you? Why are you... the way you are?'

'What do you mean?'

'You know, they way you look.'

Hephaestus shuffled awkwadly. He realised this was the first time anyone had asked him directly. It was funny. No one had asked before. He had noticed that everyone usually just took a guess rather than asking. The boy on the dock had been told he was cursed. The problem was...

'I don't know myself,' said Hephaestus, letting his huge frame down onto the deck so he was now sitting next to Eleni. 'For as long as I can remember I have been like this.' He stretched out his great hands and looked at them. 'Father told me it was a disease, but I've looked through every medical book and I can't find anything that even comes close to describing what's happened to me. All I know is that I can't remember being anything else.'

'Does your brother know?'

'Ludwig? No. We've only known about each other for about a year now. Father never told Ludwig about me and he kept me hidden. Ludwig only found out by accident and even then father lied and said I had died.'

'It sounds like there's a story there,' said Eleni and Hephaestus told her and Desses about his life in the castle cellars and about running away.

'Ludwig found you?' asked Eleni.

'That's right.'

'You must have been a shock.'

Hephaestus snorted. 'You should have seen his face. I think he nearly died of fright.'

Eleni laughed and Desses got up. 'I'm going to sleep,' he said. 'See you tomorrow.'

Eleni and Hephaestus both said good night and watched Desses disappear below deck. Once he had gone, they both sat in silence for a short time while Eleni ate.

'I'm... I'm sorry about your mother,' said Hephaestus.

'I– it was a shock,' began Eleni, 'but I always thought I would walk in and find her that way sometime. I loved her, but she didn't take care of herself or choose her friends well and... well you saw what happened.' They were quiet for a time, then Eleni asked: 'What about your family?'

'You've met my father,' said Hephaestus.

'And your mother?'

'She's dead I suppose,' said Hephaestus. 'Father never told me himself but Ludwig has asked. She must have died when Ludwig was born.'

'But aren't you older than Ludwig? Can't you remember her?'

'No, it's strange. I really can't. I think the disease that changed me also affected my memory.'

'That's sad,' said Eleni.

Hephaestus shrugged. 'Maybe, but I don't feel that way. I didn't know her so there's nothing to miss, whereas...' He glanced at Eleni. 'Sorry.'

'It's okay. When I find this Grilsgarter and the man that did that to mum, I'm going to rip their hearts out. That'll make me feel better.'

While most of the other deckhands were sleeping and Hephaestus and Eleni were talking on deck, Ludwig, deep in the bowels of the ship, decided to go wandering and to be alone. He had spent most of the day apologising and explaining to those he knew on board who he was and how he now felt awful.

He came to one of the smaller, out-of-the-way tunnels and sat down. Then he reached into his pocket, pulled out a pouch and let the little HELOT scamper onto the floor while he thought about what had happened today.

His father had been caught, which was good news of course, but a new terror had arisen that Ludwig could barely understand. He wondered whether this is what life would be like from now on. Another person finding out how to make HELOTs and using them for their own evil purposes. Ludwig shuddered at the thought. He wished they had never been created.

He was suddenly brought out of his thoughts when he no longer felt the little HELOT tugging on is finger with the piece of string. He looked down and too his horror saw it had gone.

No!

Ludwig looked left and right but there was no sign of it. Taking a blind guess at the direction, he got on his hands and knees and crawled through the tunnel as fast as he could.

Where are you!

He turned a corner and something moved up ahead.

There!

He scampered on. Right at the end of the tunnel he was lucky enough to see a glint of metal disappear through a hatch.

Wait!

Ludwig crawled as fast as he could. When he came to the small hatch that led from the tunnels to the ship proper, he pushed at it and barrelled into the next room.

'It remembers me,' said a voice from across the room.

Ludwig looked up. His father was sitting in a cell with the little HELOT in his hand.

'Beautiful isn't it? A true marvel.' Mandrake turned and looked at Ludwig. 'Come closer, my boy. Let me see your face.'

Ludwig took a few cautious steps forward. He was shaking and his mouth was dry. He didn't need this on top of everything else.

'Ah, you are growing,' said his father. 'Another year or so and I won't recognise you.'

Ludwig was silent. He couldn't think of a single thing to say. The last time he had been alone in the company of his father he had shot him; twice. If he hadn't been such a bad shot his father would have died in the Superbus' palace months ago.

'You... you won't have that long,' Ludwig managed.

Mandrake let out a small, humourless laugh. 'Maybe not, but the future is always uncertain.' He got up and moved his hand holding the little HELOT through the bars of his cell. Ludwig edged forward, grabbed it and quickly put it back in his pocket.

'Hephaestus built that you know,' said Mandrake. 'It was his first. I brought him a mouse from one of the traps in the cellars and asked him to keep it alive. I gave him a few ideas, but everything else was his.'

'And he made the HELOT?' asked Ludwig.

Mandrake laughed. 'Not straight away. Hephaestus is very bright but not *that* bright. No, it took him years to work out how to do it, but that thing in your pocket was his first success. Oh, he's such a gentle soul. He mourned every creature that died. There must be a tiny graveyard down in the cellars for each and every mouse I brought to him.'

'You're cruel,' said Ludwig quietly.

Mandrake regarded his son. 'There's worse than me, boy. Much worse.'

'I doubt it.'

'The world is a cruel place, surely you've learned that by now?'

'Grilsgarter... He just walked over those people in Nikolis Square like they weren't there.'

'Aliester is one of them. He never used to be but his

ambition has grown over the years. Now he's obsessed and nothing else matters. It's quite sad.'

For some reason the image of Rosiet lying in the dirty bed came back to Ludwig. He remembered Eleni's cries and a lump appeared in his throat. 'Can you tell me about my mother?' he asked.

'Your mother certainly wasn't one of the bad people,' said Mandrake softly. He paused to collect his words. 'She was… beautiful and kind, and very clever too.' Mandrake continued telling Ludwig about his mother until there was a noise in the corridor outside. Someone was coming.

'I have to go,' said Ludwig quietly, holding back the tears.

'So you do,' replied his father. 'It was good to see you again, my boy.'

Ludwig nodded and disappeared back into the tunnels.

Chapter Twenty: Mauraders

'Mother!'

Aliester Grilsgarter's voice echoed down the corridors of his home. He had been running for two days nonstop and now he was covered in dust and his joints creaked. But he had done it! He had what they wanted!

'What's is it, my sweetness?' came a reply.

Aliester bent down and walked into the main hall of the villa. His mother sat at the other end of the room and in her hands were a pair of needles clicking together furiously.

'I have the plans!' Aliester cried. 'I have them!'

'My cherished one, my light, well done!'

Aliester strode the length of the hall, his huge body scraping against the upper rafters as he passed, upsetting the spiders that lived there. When he got to his mother, his body folded down so that his dead face hung next to her. His mother looked into the cold black lenses where her son's eyes used to be.

'Yes, mother! Look, look!' Grilsgarter's mechanical claw reached out and passed his mother the sheets of crumpled paper he had held so tightly.

Lady Beatrice Grilsgarter flicked through them quickly. Her eyes lit up. It was Mandrake von Guggenstein's handwriting, and what was written looked correct. 'Oh, my darling one.' She stood up and kissed her son on his clammy forehead. 'You did well, my sweetness. You've made mother very proud. We will begin at once.'

She swept out of the room with her son trailing behind.

After Ludwig had spoken to his father, he ran back through the tunnels to the cabin the Captain had given him. He lay on his bed wide awake until late thinking about what his father had said. When sleep came, he dreamt of his brother working away in the cellars, building the little wonder that was currently resting in the drawer beside him. He also dreamt of the mother he and his brother never knew. But his dreams didn't last long.

Crack!

It was still dark when Ludwig rubbed his eyes and reached for the lamp nearby, letting light flicker into the cabin. It must have been only two or three in the morning and he guessed he had slept for only a few hours. Something had woken him but he had no idea what.

Crack!

There was a noise from the corridor outside followed by a cry. Ludwig recognised the noise. It was a gunshot. He jumped out of bed, but as he pulled on a dressing gown a slow, creaking sound came from the other side of the room. He looked up to see the handle of his door turn.

'What's going on?' he called out fearfully.

There was no reply as the door opened. Behind was a man Ludwig didn't recognise. In his hand was a pistol.

'What have we got here?' snarled the man as he walked into Ludwig's cabin. 'A young 'un, eh? You best come with me.'

Behind the man Ludwig heard shouting and screaming in the corridor. More gunshots went off. It sounded like a war was going on in the ship that had come from nowhere.

'Who *are* you? What's going on?' Ludwig shouted.

'Just a bit of business, lad. Now you be good and come along.' The man gestured for Ludwig to leave the cabin with his pistol.

Knowing there was nowhere to run, Ludwig walked past the man and went outside. The man followed.

In the corridor, Ludwig saw people fighting. The *Kamaria's* crew and Sir Notsworth's Companions were clashing with men Ludwig didn't recognise. Many lay on the floor, groaning or silent. For a brief moment he thought he was dreaming still. None of this seemed real.

Nearby, Ludwig spotted Senka. Another man stood next to him holding a pistol in his hand.

'What's happening?' asked Ludwig quietly when he was closer.

'Dunno,' said Senka. 'They came out of nowhere. There's fightin' all over the ship! I— I think they're here for your dad. I heard one of them sayin' they're lookin' for 'im. They're rounding up the deckhands too for some reason.'

'Shut it,' said the man who had found Ludwig, hitting Senka hard around the head and making him cry out. The man glanced towards the fighting and then back at the two boys. 'This way,' he said, pointing his pistol in the other direction.

Ludwig and Senka began making their way down the corridor and the two men followed behind.

'We need to get away,' Ludwig whispered to Senka, remembering when Jack had kidnapped him from Galleesha. He never wanted to be someone's prisoner ever again.

'The ship's tunnels,' Senka whispered back. He looked a few feet along the corridor and there was one of the hatches. 'They shouldn't follow us so easily in there.'

The two boys slowly walked down the corridor, but just before they got to the stairway, Ludwig and Senka dived left through one of the hatches and into the deckhands' tunnels. There was a shout of anger in the corridor behind them.

'Split up!' shouted Ludwig and without pausing Senka ran in one direction and Ludwig the other.

The tunnel Ludwig found himself in was one of the bigger ones. He could run almost standing as long as he kept his head down. He sped off as quickly as he could. Any tiredness that had stayed with him from when he awoke had fled, but behind he could hear someone following him. There was a cry as whoever it was bashed their head against the ceiling. The deckhands' tunnels were meant for deckhands only. Anyone older and taller was going to have a terrible time.

Ludwig ran on, hoping above all else the men weren't able to catch up. He darted around the corner and then shot right. He saw another hatch. He jumped through it and found himself in the galley. Looking around, he ran to the counter where the knives were kept. A few were missing but the meat cleaver was still there. He grabbed it then hid behind the pantry door.

At the other end of the room the hatch opened again and Ludwig heard his pursuer enter. The man was cursing loudly and Ludwig guessed he must have a sore head. Ludwig ducked down, holding the cleaver tight and tried to stop breathing in case the man heard.

'I know yer in here,' said the man as Ludwig's legs started to shake. 'We've got the ship. You can't hide forever.'

Ludwig heard the floor creak.

'I bet I can guess where you are.'

The floor boards creaked again. Closer this time.

Ludwig braced himself. If he was fast enough, he thought, he could jump out and get the man before he had a chance to fire.

If he was fast enough.

Ludwig closed his eyes, counted to three, and held the cleaver up high.

He ran.

'Argh-!' Ludwig cried out, sprinting around the pantry door and towards where he had heard the man standing. Suddenly there was a bang. Ludwig felt the cleaver fly out of his hands and clatter into a corner nearby and then something heavy hit the floor with a grunt. He opened his eyes and on the floor of the galley Ludwig saw the man who had taken him from his cabin. He was dead. Ludwig had no idea how.

Strange...

He sniffed and could smell gun powder. He went over to the man, looked at his pistol, and felt the barrel. It had been fired and there had been one bang, which meant the bullet that had knocked the cleaver out of Ludwig's hands had come from his pursuers gun.

Ludwig breathed in. That had been far too close. But...who killed the man? There was no one else here! More gunshots from the ship brought Ludwig to his senses. There was no time to wonder who had helped him for now. While trying not to think how close he had come to being shot, he ran out of the galley and into the corridors once again.

Outside, Ludwig could see the ship was a mess. Bullet holes riddled the walls and men lay slumped on the floor, dark pools spreading beneath them.

One of the crew ran past and Ludwig caught hold of him. 'Where's the Captain?' Ludwig called out.

'Don't know!' replied the man. 'He went to bed a few hours ago. His door's locked and these blighters are trying to get in. He must sleep like the dead to have missed this!'

Ludwig nodded to the man and dived into another set of tunnels. A few minutes later he burst out again and into the Captain's quarters.

When Ludwig arrived he cried out in surprise upon seeing the captain standing at the back of the room, perfectly still. There was something about it that sent a shiver down his spine. Ludwig guessed with all that was going on the Captain had forgotten to lock the hatch to the tunnels when he went to sleep. Ludwig had been lucky to find them open and glad no one else had discovered the Captain this way.

'Captain!' Ludwig called out. 'Wake up, *please!* We're being attacked!'

The Captain didn't move.

On the other side of the room Ludwig heard the door being tried then someone started banging on it. They were trying to get in!

Ludwig ran up to the Captain and took hold of one of his hands. He started to shake it. The door was creaking dangerously now and there was shouting outside. Ludwig was terrified but he kept on shaking the Captain and shouting.

'Wake up! Captain! *Please!* Wake up!'

Feeling hopeless as cracks appeared in the cabin door, Ludwig slumped onto the floor.

'Captain...'

Ludwig felt something. He looked up and saw the Captain's fingers jerk. He looked at the Captain's face and saw light returning to the Captain's eyes.

'You're awake!' cried Ludwig.

The Captain looked down. 'Ludwig? What are yer doin' here? What's going on?'

'We're under attack!' cried Ludwig. He pointed to the door that was now almost off its hinges. 'Look!'

The Captain took one look at the door then turned and ran to the other side of the room. His other body was there, the one Hephaestus had made in Galleesha when he had first died. It was huge, with powerful crushing arms and covered in strong patterned armour with bronze skulls where each arm met. Next to the body was a man-shaped space.

'Stand back,' said the Captain. 'I've not done this before. Hephaestus showed me what to do but it might scare you a bit.'

Ludwig nodded and stayed where he was.

The Captain went up to the space, turned, and stepped backwards. There was a hiss as two clamps came down onto his shoulders and from behind the Captain's head, Ludwig heard a grinding sound. A second later the lights in the Captain's smaller body died. He unscrewed his head from his body, lifted it up and then placed it onto his other body. The grinding sound was heard again and there was a hiss.

The Captain's eyes grew bright again.

Unfortunately, it was at this point that Hephaestus' workshop door burst open and the invaders ran in.

They ran out again very quickly.

When he got onto deck, Hephaestus saw the fighting was even more furious than below. He too had been asleep when the invaders attacked. He had jumped out of bed, hit the alarm to wake the Captain, and went outside hoping the Captain's start-up wouldn't take too long. Then he crashed through the corridors towards Ludwig's cabin, but it had been empty. *The deck,* he had thought. *They've taken him!*

Once out in the open air, he smashed into the first man he didn't recognise without pausing, driving the man to the floor and leaving him unconscious before swinging his fist at another. As he picked himself up he looked to his left and there stood Eleni and Desses swiping at the invaders. Near their feet were the remains of those that had got too close.

'Are you okay?' Hephaestus called out.

Eleni looked up at Hephaestus and winked. She sprang into the air, only just missing the blade of one her attackers. As she came down again three invaders fell. Hephaestus was impressed, but he could also see things were looking hopeless. For every invader they stopped, two more took their place. And they had nowhere to run.

Where's the Captain?! Hephaestus thought to himself. But it was dawning on him that he knew what they would have to do.

'Eleni!' he cried out, still pushing the attackers away. 'I think we have to sur–'

There was a deep rumbling sound to Hephaestus' right. As he forced another man off the side of the *Kamaria*, he turned.

The Captain burst from below.

'My gods!' cried those on deck as the Captain reared up in his new body. Both crew and invaders alike gasped.

'It's an 'ELOT!' cried one of the crew. 'They've got an 'ELOT! We're doomed!'

'No! Wait!' Hephaestus cried back. 'It's the Captain!'

The crew saw the creature grab the nearest invader and throw them overboard.

'Pull the other one it's got bells on!' cried the crewman.

'Trust me,' Hephaestus replied with a mangled grin. 'It's him!' Hephaestus waved at the Captain and the Captain waved back. The crew let out a cheer.

'It's me, mates,' the Captain called out. 'Apologies for springin' this on yer. Once this is over, I'll explain everythin', I promise.'

The invaders fell back as the Captain advanced. Many ran, screaming. The crew looked at one another. It was good enough for them. They started fighting again with the taste of victory in their mouths as the Captain fought his way over to Hephaestus.

'You all right?' the Captain asked.

'Yes,' Hephaestus replied, breathing heavily. 'But who are they? They came out of nowhere!'

'Hang on,' said the Captain. He reached out and grabbed the nearest invader, scrunching the man's shirt in his fist and lifting him up. 'What are yer doin' 'ere?' he asked pointedly.

'We're here on a job!' cried the man. 'We're here for Mandrake and some boy called Ludwig! Lord Pashymore sent us!'

Below, Sir Notsworth stood in the brig with his back to the cells. In front of him the invaders were trying to get through the narrow door that led into the rest of the ship. They poured into the room, pushing Sir Notsworth and his men back.

'There he is!' shouted one of the invaders when he caught sight of their prize. 'Mandrake's in here!'

'You dog!' cried Sir Notsworth, firing his pistol at the man who had called out. The man ducked out of sight as the wood above him splintered.

Around Sir Notsworth were his Companions. Each one was fighting and Sir Notsworth couldn't help but notice they seemed to be enjoying themselves immensely. Killer held one invader in his hands and had started using the poor fellow as a club to attack the others; while Gu'Liok was simply a blur, the invaders barely seeing him before they fell. Sir Notsworth had known him long enough to stay well back while he got on with it.

Another invader popped up and Sir Notsworth swung at him. 'Have at you, sir!' he cried, striking out with his rapier. The invader parried it with ease and grinned.

'Oh, it's like that is it?' said Sir Notsworth. 'The impudence!'

With a battle cry he remembered from his old school days, Sir Notsworth surged forward and the invader's grin quickly faded. While Sir Notsworth was getting a little slow in his old age, he'd had more duels than he could remember and his experience shone through. The invader dropped his sword and ran out of the room, pushing his own men out of the way in the process, terrified of the raging aristocrat.

'Ha!' cried Sir Notsworth before ducking as another man slashed at him. 'Great days! And you can tell your master we'll not have a Petraya back on the throne, I can guarantee you that!'

While Sir Notsworth and his Companions continued fighting, there was an almighty crash outside followed by a lot of screaming. The invaders in the brig looked back and upon seeing their friends flee, threw down their own weapons and ran as well.

'That's right,' shouted Sir Notsworth. 'You'd better run – Oh.'

The Captain appeared in the doorway. He had to bend down to get through, and Ludwig was in the crook of his arm. At least Sir Notsworth guessed it was Ludwig since all he could see was the boy's backside.

'Hello Captain,' said Sir Notsworth. 'Is that Ludwig you have there?'

'Hullo, Notsworth,' said Ludwig, trying to wave behind him.

'Ah, good to see you are alive and well. Captain, we kept the curs at bay. Mandrake remains safe.'

'Good,' said the Captain. 'They were here for him.'

'Grilsgarter wants him back, eh?'

'No,' said the Captain, sounding furious. 'Pashymore did.'

'*What?*'

'The damned idiot really did hire bounty hunters,' the Captain boomed.

Eventually the Captain cleared the *Kamaria* of the bounty hunters and the ship was safe again. As they marched through the ship, the Captain couldn't help but feel better despite the chaos as Sir Notsworth graphically told of all the things he would do to Lord Pashymore once he saw him again. Once they were done and guards were posted, they went to the crew's quarters.

'Captain,' said one of the crewmen when they entered.

'I'm afraid close to thirty are down.'

The Captain went to one corner, picked up a bucket, and threw the water over himself to wash away the fight. Then he looked over the crew's quarters. It was full of wounded crewmen. Others not so badly hurt in the fighting stood with them, helping as much as possible.

'Where's Yoddette?' asked the Captain. 'He should be here.'

The crewman shook his head. 'Doc's dead, Captain.'

'Blast! I can't lose this many!'

The door opened again and Hephaestus walked in with Ludwig and Eleni behind him.

'There is someone who could help,' said Hephaestus.

The Captain turned. 'No.'

'I don't like it either but he knows what he's doing. I'll watch him myself.'

The Captain looked around the room. A couple of crewmen were standing over a cot. They looked up, caught the Captain's eye, and one shook his head. Then they moved to the next man and did the same.

'We're losing them,' said Hephaestus.

The Captain balled up his fists. 'Get him,' he growled.

Hephaestus left and soon returned with Mandrake. Mandrake was still shackled as he looked around the room.

'A tragic situation,' he said, going over to the first crewman that was still alive. 'You have needle and thread?' he asked. One of crew looked at the Captain, then nodded and passed the items to Mandrake.

'Thank you. Please, hold him down.'

Mandrake worked quickly. Once he was done he turned back to the Captain. 'He'll live. Please, Leave me here. I'll do what I can. Hephaestus can watch me.'

The Captain thought for a while then nodded. 'Fine, but you do *anythin'* suspicious and you're back in the brig again.'

'Of course.'

The Captain considered his ship. They had lost a lot of men and there was a lot of damage. He was amazed they were still afloat.

'How far away are we?' he asked Mandrake.

Mandrake looked up and out of a port hole. 'I'd say a day or two, no more.'

'Good,' replied the Captain. 'The sooner this is done with, the better. We can't survive out here much longer.'

Chapter Twenty-One:
Casa de Grilsgarter

Two days later the *Kamaria* came to a stop at a part of the riverbank Mandrake had pointed out. When the calls for weighing anchor reached the lower parts of the ship, Hephaestus left the repairs he had been making and went up on deck. There, he saw his father standing looking out over the rolling hills.

It was quiet here, with no people and no buildings in view. The only signs of life were the grazing cattle and the dirt paths that criss-crossed the land. The Captain and Sir Notsworth stood nearby.

'This is it,' said Mandrake, leaning against the railing. It's a few hours walk that way.' He pointed. 'I'll show you–'

'You're staying *right* here,' said the Captain firmly, 'but I *do* need t'know where we're goin' and what I should expect. He put a piece of paper and a charcoal stick on the railing. 'Just draw what I need to know.'

Mandrake took the paper and charcoal. He drew the plan of a villa and marked the entrance to it with an X.

'You can get inside this way,' said Mandrake pointing at the front of the villa. 'There might be a few guards hidden away but they shouldn't cause a problem. Grilsgarter isn't expecting anyone.'

'There's no other way?' asked the Captain. 'We just go through the front door?'

'Trust me,' said Mandrake.

The Captain left an hour later. He took with him all the crew and Companions that could still walk and hold a rifle, just in case this wouldn't be quite as easy as Mandrake suggested. Hephaestus knew the Captain had good reason not to trust his father, and for all they knew Grilsgarter could have an army with him. Hephaestus and Sir Notsworth came along too, leaving Eleni to look after the ship.

As they travelled to Grilsgarter's home they had kept away from the roads and paths, away from prying eyes; just to be safe. Both Hephaestus and the Captain had heard the Painted Man tell them Grilsgarter did not want to be found and they could guess the lengths he would go to in order to keep his privacy.

While they walked, Hephaestus remembered Ludwig's face as they were getting off the *Kamaria*. Ludwig hadn't wanted to come along with them *this* time.

'Be careful,' was all Ludwig had said, pale-faced before Hephaestus had boarded the longboat to carry them ashore.

Hephaestus then remembered Eleni. She had been a different story. The only reason she was here, she had said, was to kill whoever had murdered her mother. But finally, after much convincing she agreed to stay behind.

'I'll send for you, love,' the Captain had said. 'But I want to make sure it's safe first. That's all we're doin'.'

By the time they arrived at Grilsgarter's villa it was quiet and night was approaching. The villa itself was a large low building covered in verandas and shuttered windows, and surrounded by exquisitely maintained gardens. Mandrake had been right about the guards too. There were none keeping watch and the place looked deserted. All that kept the Captain's party out was a high wall that ran around the front of the estate although here and there were gates set into it that nobody seemed to have bothered to lock.

One of the crewmen approached the Captain and

Hephaestus' hiding place. He had been sent to scout ahead 'It looks clear,' said the crewman. 'But Mandrake were right, there's no other way in.'

'We're ready,' said the Captain. 'Hephaestus, Notsworth, stay close to me.'

The Captain signalled and the crew and Sir Notsworth's companions entered through one of the gates, taking up positions behind the bushes in the garden beyond.

'No sign of movement yet, sir,' hissed Sir Notsworth.

'Keep your eyes open,' said the Captain. 'I don't like this. And you don't have to call me "sir".'

'I know,' whispered Sir Notsworth. 'But it seems appropriate. Plus I can blame you if anything goes wrong.'

They kept moving towards the main entrance of the villa, keeping low. When they got closer, the Captain called Hephaestus and Sir Notsworth to him.

'I'll go first to see if there's any trouble. Stay well behind me.'

Hephaestus and Sir Notsworth nodded.

The Captain reached out and pushed the door open. It creaked loudly as he made his way in. On the other side of the door was a small dark room and set into the far wall was another set of doors. The Captain crept through the room slowly. He looked up, but there was nothing to suggest an ambush. Behind him, he heard Hephaestus and Sir Notsworth come in with the rest following.

When he got to the doors, he reached out and pulled but the door wouldn't budge. Using all his strength, the Captain broke the door from its hinges.

There was nothing but a wall behind the door.

'Get back!' the Captain cried, turning quickly and flinging the door aside. 'It's a trap! It's a blasted trap. Mandrake–!'

It was too late. A block of stone crashed down where the first set of doors had been, trapping them inside. Some unfortunate souls were caught underneath and Hephaestus had to look away.

'I appear to have guests,' came a voice; high and shrill. 'However, I am quite certain you weren't invited. Please brace yourselves.'

'Wha–?' began Hephaestus, but he couldn't finish. The floor suddenly fell away.

The Captain, Hephaestus, Sir Notsworth and the crew that had made it inside fell into an inky blackness. The last thing Hephaestus felt before he lost consciousness was the floor below coming to meet him.

Outside the villa, the world exploded. Grilsgarter's men appeared everywhere; on all the villa's balconies and on every rooftop. They poured into the garden through hidden doors and out of fox holes in the garden lawn.

'Fall back!' Gu'liok cried out, raising his rifle and firing. 'Fall back now!'

'We can't,' said Killer, standing beside him. He looked grimly over the garden. 'It looks like it's fightin' or dyin' time fer us.'

Gu'loik looked back to see the gates had swung shut. Some of the Companions and crew were trying to open them, but they held fast. He looked back at Killer.

'We might as well get thissss over and done with,' said Gu'liok. 'First to fifty sssscalps gets a bottle of the good sssstuff on the other side?'

Killer smiled at him. 'Fifty? Make it a hundred.'

Gu'loik smiled back and flung himself into the fight. Killer was on his heels. Grilsgarter's men swarmed and the battle begun in earnest.

Chapter Twenty-Two: Sons and Fathers

'Wake up.'

Hephaestus groaned and his head hurt. He knew he was lying down but when he tried to move he felt the cold metal of chains around his wrists. He moved so he was sitting up, the shackles were slack enough to allow that, but he couldn't go any further. He lifted his head.

No...

In front of him was the creature he had seen at Beacon docks months before: Aliester Grilsgarter. Hephaestus felt ill even looking at him. Grilsgarter's human body hung limply from the skeletal machine to which it was attached, with only a few drapes of cloth to stop it being completely naked. Its mouth hung open with a speaker lodged in its throat where that rasping voice emerged, and its eyes were black whirring pits, glass lenses without feeling. A few wisps of hair hung down over his face and through thin skin Hephaestus could see veins and muscles. Grilsgarter also stank. The smell was truly awful.

Hephaestus quickly looked around. They were in a cellar that he guessed was under the villa. Grilsgarter was even able to stand up straight down here. Then he spied an archway in one wall, with stairs leading upwards. A way out.

'So you must be Hephaestus von Guggenstein,' said Grilsgarter. 'I've heard a great deal about you from your father.'

There was a groan nearby. Hephaestus ignored Grilsgarter, turned, and saw Sir Notsworth on the floor; in chains like him.

'Ah,' said Grilsgarter. 'Our other guests are waking up.'

'Oh, my head!' muttered Sir Notsworth. He opened his eyes and looked about. 'Where are we? Hephaestus, is that you?' He then saw Grilsgarter. 'By Azmon...' he managed but his voice failed him.

'Sir Notsworth O'Reilly,' said Grilsgarter. 'I am sorry to put you in this predicament, sir.'

'What?' said Sir Notsworth, astonished. 'You know me?'

'Of course!' said Grilsgarter. 'I've read your books too. Quite an adventurer aren't you? I'm something of a fan.'

'Then let us go, blast it!' shouted Sir Notsworth, jiggling his chains.

'That I cannot do I'm afraid.'

Hephaestus then heard the Captain's voice echo in the dungeon. 'Leave 'em alone!'

Hephaestus looked back to see the Captain pinned to the back wall. Great metal bands covered his limbs, keeping him in place.

Grilsgarter stepped past Hephaestus and walked over to the Captain.

'Incredible,' he whined. 'My own body is clearly very old fashioned these days. It's very embarrassing. Hephaestus, did you do this?'

Hephaestus couldn't believe it. 'How could you know that?'

'Your father sent us lots of letters before the... unpleasantness in Beacon. He told me of your invention. Very impressive. Your father tried for years without success. Now, I have a question: Why have you come here?'

'To stop you,' said Hephaestus.

'To stop me?' Grilsgarter replied. 'To stop me doing what? Has Mandrake told you why I wanted him?'

'We know you want to build HELOTs.'

Grilsgarter laughed. It was awful, a high-pitched screech that bounced off the walls. 'Is that what you think? That I took your father because I wanted *HELOTs?*'

'But he said...'

'It sounds like your father hasn't given you the whole truth,' said Grilsgarter.

'You're a Petraya,' said Hephaestus. 'You want the throne again.'

'Yes, you're right. I *am* a Petraya, but I have no interest in thrones or empires. I don't want an army, Hephaestus, and I never have.'

'But the letter. Father promised...'

'Your father was not going to give me an army, Hephaestus. Power was always *his* obsession; that and revenge of course. All that death and destruction just to attack Galleesha for something that had happened years ago. I think he took an interest in my family for the same reason. I expect he thought we would take up arms and bring back the old empire. But the old empire is finished, and good riddance. No, I wanted something different.'

Hephaestus was confused. It had all made sense hadn't it? This creature wanted an army. *Everyone* wanted an army like that. 'Then... then why did you kidnap him?' he asked.

'It's very simple,' replied Grilsgarter. 'He promised me an heir. I didn't want him to die before I had that.'

'What?'

'Hephaestus, do you know how I came to be the creature that stands before you, or did your father lie about that too?'

'He didn't say anything to me,' said Hephaestus.

'He said you were attacked instead of him,' said Sir Notsworth, remembering what Mandrake had said on the *Kamaria*

'That's right. The Petrayas are an important family. My... change meant I couldn't have children. In all honesty, I am not so concerned, but it is important to mother.'

'Mother?'

'Oh, this was all mother's idea really. Alas, she is getting old and can no longer have children of her own. She was so upset when Mandrake changed me.'

'But... I don't understand,' said Hephaestus. 'How can father help you with an heir?'

'Hephaestus, where do you think you come from?' asked Grilsgarter.

'What?'

'Where were you born? Who is your mother? Why are you... well, the way you are? Mandrake never told you, did he? You have no idea. Your father achieved something quite extraordinary and you are completely in the dark. Let me show you.'

There was a table against one wall. Grilsgarter went over to it, took something, and dropped it in front of Hephaestus. It was a letter.

'Read it,' said Grilsgarter.

Hephaestus took the envelope and read.

Grilsgarter,

The experiments go well. The first five passed away, but the sixth has stayed alive. He is a perfect child. He grows well and will be stronger and more intelligent than any other human that has walked on this world.

We must wait a few years to make sure all is well but the template is there. You shall have your heir and we shall be even.

Mandrake

'What was he doing...?' rumbled Hephaestus.

'Now read this,' said Grilsgarter, passing Hephaestus

another letter. Hephaestus took it dumbly. Terrible thoughts began to burrow into his brain.

> *Grilsgarter,*
>
> *I have bad news. The child has changed. It has become a monster! I have saved its mind but its body had been lost forever. However, we must not despair. I tried too hard, that is all. Perhaps a perfect creature is not possible. The next will be more stable I am sure of it.*
>
> *Mandrake.*

'This child...' began Hephaestus. His voice trembled.

'Whatever those letters say, mate,' said the Captain. 'Don't believe it. Stop readin'.'

'This is the final letter I received from your father,' said Grilsgarter, passing it to Hephaestus.

> *Grilsgarter,*
>
> *Child seven has not changed. A few more years are needed to confirm the results, but it looks very promising. I will send you instructions soon.*
>
> *Mandrake.*

Hephaestus put the letter down.

'Child seven is Ludwig,' said Grilsgarter.

'Then...' said Hephaestus."

'You are child six.'

'They've been gone a long time,' said Ludwig looking out over the railing of *Kamaria*.

It was evening now and no one on the *Kamaria Pili* had heard anything from the Captain or his party. They should have been back hours ago, or at least sent word. Ludwig, Eleni, Senka, and Desses stood on deck, looking at the shore and hoping to catch sight of them.

Suddenly Ludwig spotted something moving on the riverbank. He ran to the ship's wheel, grabbed the Captain's spy glass and looked again. On the far beach he could just about make out a man waving to the *Kamaria* and trying to drag one of the longboats back into the water. Ludwig could see he was struggling. He barely moved the boat a few feet before he fell into the sand. Even as he laid on the ground, he weakly pushed on the boat, desperate to get back to the ship.

'One of the crew is out there!' Ludwig cried to the others on deck.

Eleni took the spy-glass and looked through it, then she ordered two of the remaining crew to get a longboat into the water. She jumped into it with Desses and they rowed to the beach, picked up the man and brought him back. Once they were on the *Kamaria* again the exhausted sailor spoke.

'It were a trap!' he whimpered. 'The captain, the big 'un, and Sir Notsworth. They were taken!'

'What happened to the rest?' asked Eleni.

'We were attacked from all sides! It were a massacre. I only just got out...so many fell...'

'Did anyone else get away?' asked Ludwig.

The crewman shook his head. 'No, I don't think so. No one else. Just me. Just *me.*'

Eleni looked at those on deck. The few that had been left behind were gathering as news of the returned crewman spread. She thought about a rescue party, but the crew who had been left behind were too injured to fight after the attack by the bounty hunters. And the few deckhands would be no use against Grilsgarter's men.

'What do you think we should do?' asked Ludwig.

'I'm going after them,' said Eleni.

'Then I'm coming too.'

'You?' said Eleni. 'You'll just get killed.'

'He's got my brother and my friends. You can't stop me.'

Eleni regarded Ludwig quietly. She then pulled a pistol from her belt and handed it to him.

'Fine. You're going to need one of these.'

Chapter Twenty-Three:
A Stern Line

'Do you know who you are?' continued Grilsgarter as Hephaestus lay slumped on the floor. 'You and Ludwig are copies of Mandrake's own father. His death has always played on Mandrake's mind and I suppose he saw this as a way of getting him back. No wonder Mandrake was so obsessed with Ludwig during the Terror. I imagine losing his father twice would be too much for him to bear.'

'Stop it man!' cried Sir Notsworth. 'Hephaestus, he's lying to you lad! Don't listen! I don't know what he's trying to do, but it's not true!'

The Captain shouted much the same thing.

'No,' muttered Hephaestus. 'He's right. It all makes sense. Ludwig and I are the same person.'

'No yer not, mate!' said the Captain. 'And so what if you are? You're still you.'

'Father did this to me,' said Hephaestus, rising, looking at his monstrous body. 'He *made* this!'

Hephaestus' roar echoed through the villa.

Eleni pushed open the door to the brig and went to Mandrake's cell. Mandrake was sitting eating stale bread. He looked up when he heard Eleni.

'They've not come back, have they?' he asked.

Eleni ignored him and unlocked the door.

'Get out.'

Eleni took Mandrake to the deck with her pistol at his

back. They found the others standing around a table covered in pistols, rifles, and sabres.

'Ludwig? Is this your plan?' asked Mandrake. 'A bunch of children and invalids attempting to fight.'

'The wounded and the children are staying here,' Ludwig replied. 'It's just me, you and Eleni.'

'Me?' said Mandrake.

'You know where Grilsgarter lives,' said Ludwig flatly.

'Quite,' replied his father. He looked out over the boat to the shore. 'But Grilsgarter will kill you if you go to his home. This is not Beacon boy; and you are not facing me this time.'

'He's not going alone,' said Eleni. She turned to the crewman that had come back. 'Say again what happened?'

The crewman explained about how the Captain, Hephaestus, and Sir Notsworth were captured.

'You knew that would happen didn't you?' said Ludwig.

'No,' said Mandrake. 'I told your Captain the truth.'

'Liar!' shouted Ludwig. He felt strange. Cold. And very, very angry.

'Let me handle this,' said Eleni. She went over to the table, picked up a pistol and walked over to Mandrake. 'Desses, hold him,' she ordered.

Desses grabbed Mandrake from behind. Then he took one of Mandrake's hands and held it down against the railing.

'What are you doing?' cried Mandrake. 'Ludwig, tell them to let go of me!'

Ludwig shook his head.

'Ludwig's right, you are lying. And this is what we do to liars in Guly Porta,' said Eleni.

She raised the pistol and Ludwig turned his head. There was a shot and a scream, and Ludwig caught sight of Senka's face; it was white as snow. When Ludwig looked back at his father, Mandrake was on the floor holding his hand in the crook of his arm. He was whimpering and there was a lot of blood.

Eleni cracked open the pistol and reloaded it.

'Tell me how to help them or I'll shoot off another one. You've got ten seconds. After that I'll keep taking them until you speak. She pulled back the hammer.

'Wait!' Mandrake managed. 'There's...' he breathed deeply, trying to ignore the pain. 'There's another way in. In the hills behind the villa.'

'Dad was far too soft on you,' said Eleni. 'He should have done this from the beginning. Get up.'

'You want me to come *with* you after this?' moaned Mandrake. 'I'm bleeding!'

'Desses?' said Eleni. Desses threw Mandrake some strips of cloth. 'I saw what you did for those people after the bounty hunters attacked. I'm sure you can take care of yourself.'

While Mandrake looked after his wound, Eleni took a sabre for herself then looked at the remainder of the ship's crew.

'Make sure the ship is secure and keep watch,' said Eleni. 'We'll be back soon. Desses, look after things until then.'

The crew nodded.

'Be careful,' said Desses.

'Oh, I will,' said Eleni.

Chapter Twenty-Four:
The Birthing Pool

It was around midnight when they arrived at Grilsgarter's villa.

Ludwig peered through its gates. He had expected the villa to be cold and forbidding, but in fact it looked surprisingly homely.

'So how do we get in?' Eleni hissed at Mandrake. 'Remember: you lie and it'll be more of your fingers I'll be taking.'

'There's another entrance,' said Mandrake grudgingly. 'Follow me.'

Mandrake led them around the villa and towards a group of low hills nearby. Against one hill there was a group of boulders. Once they got to the boulders, Ludwig's father looked closely then reached in between two of them and tugged at something. There was a grinding sound and one of the larger stones rolled to one side, exposing a passage that led into the hill itself.

'Aliester is rather paranoid,' said Mandrake. He worries assassins may come to finish off his family for good. This is his means of escape.'

'Let's go,' said Eleni.

Mandrake stepped through first, but before Eleni could do anything he spun around and hit a button on the inside of the tunnel wall. The boulder suddenly rolled back, leaving Mandrake on one side and Eleni and Ludwig on the other.

'No!' screamed Eleni.

'Wait,' said Ludwig. He scrabbled around the boulder and found the lever his father had used. He pulled and the boulder rolled open again, but Mandrake had gone.

'I'm beginning to *really* hate your dad,' said Eleni.

'Just like everyone else then,' said Ludwig.

They ran down the passage towards the villa. Five minutes later, they came to another door. There was another button. Ludwig pressed it and another door slid open.

They came to a storeroom attached to a large kitchen. Eleni went first, making sure the room was clear before Ludwig came through.

'Which way?' asked Eleni.

'Your guess is as good as mine,' said Ludwig.

'Then we'll have to search the whole place,' said Eleni. 'However long it takes.'

Mandrake crept through Grilsgarter's villa, his mind churning. What was he to do? Ludwig was as good as dead now, surely. There was little chance he was going to survive in this place. It was a shame to lose the boy after all that had happened, but Mandrake had made his peace at his execution. Since he had been kidnapped by Aliester, his only thoughts were of his own survival. Nothing else mattered.

There was a noise further down the corridor and he dived into the nearest room. He turned and pressed his back against the door, letting the guards pass by.

When the guards had gone he looked around the room he found himself in. It was a bedroom. Mandrake walked over to the bed and sat down, letting himself relax.

A few minutes later his future appeared to him and he smiled.

'Of course...'

The villa itself seemed almost deserted, but they did pass a few of Grilsgarter's men occasionally. Ludwig and Eleni hid whenever they were near.

Then as they passed a door, something caught Ludwig's eye.

'Wait,' he said.

'What is it?' Eleni asked.

Ludwig ignored her and stepped through the doorway. This room was different from the rest. It was a laboratory of some sort and reminded Ludwig of his father's workshop back home. He entered and stared at the apparatus. It bubbled and fizzed while they stood there.

'We need to find my dad and stop yours,' hissed Eleni, pulling at Ludwig. 'We don't have time for sightseeing.'

But Ludwig pushed Eleni's hand away. There was something important here.

In the centre of the room was a metal egg-shaped... thing, about three times the size of a man's head. Pipes from all the nearby machines poured to it, pumping liquids.

Ludwig stepped closer.

'Don't...' said Eleni behind him. 'That thing looks wrong.'

'It's okay,' said Ludwig, mesmerized by the metallic egg. Something odd was going on, like a switch had been flicked on in his head. A ghost from the past appeared in the back of his mind.

Something about this machine seemed... *familiar*.

'Ludwig,' Eleni called. 'I'm leaving.'

Ludwig turned. 'No-'

'Oi! You!'

Ludwig and Eleni spun round. In the doorway stood a man. Eleni's eye's widened. It was the man who had escaped on the slaver's boat; the one she was sure had killed her mother on Grilsgarter's orders.

'What have we got here?' Ekhert sneered 'Are you the

rescue party? Ha, Grilsgarter will chew you up and spit you out.'

He drew his sword. 'Don't worry, I won't hurt yer much. He doesn't like his toys cut up before he's had a chance to play with them.'

'Ludwig, hide,' said Eleni, drawing her own sword and moving between the man and the boy.

Ludwig darted behind the table with the metal egg on it as Eleni pounced. Ludwig huddled down. He heard the crash of metal against metal. It carried on for a minute or so and he could here Ekhert grunt, first in surprise, then in determination. Eleni made no sound.

'I know you,' said Eleni as she circled the man.

'I don't think so,' said Ekhert.

'Can't you see it in my face? Look closely. Do you remember my mother Rosiet'

'Ah, I can see the family resemblance,' said Ekhert. 'I'm sorry she died.'

'You killed her.'

'Yes I did, and if I didn't Grilsgarter would have killed me. You would have done the same.'

'Murderer!' Eleni ran forward and lashed out. Ekhert fell back from her onslaught.

'You've got some fight in you, I'll give you that–'

There was a sickening, ripping sound and Ekhert looked down. 'How?' He managed before slumping to the floor.

From behind the table, Ludwig felt something wet on his hand. He looked down and saw blood running through the grooves between the tiles on the floor. He quickly pulled his hand away.

'You can come out now,' said Eleni.

Ludwig stood up and saw Eleni standing over Ekhert. Ekhert wasn't moving and the floor glistened.

'Do you feel better?' asked Ludwig quietly.

Eleni stared at Ekhert's body.

'Yes,' said Eleni. 'But it won't bring mum back.'

'No,' said Ludwig. 'Come on, we-'

Ludwig was about to take a step forward but stopped dead. Something inside the egg had caught his eye.

Eleni wiped down her sword and looked up. She saw Ludwig was staring at a small window in the side of the egg. She gasped. Something was staring back...

Chapter Twenty-Five: Old Friends

'It's been a long time Beatrice.'

Beatrice Grilsgarter was finishing decorating her hair when she heard that voice. Her hands stopped dead.

'*It can't be.* 'Mandrake... is that you?''

Mandrake slid out of the shadows of Beatrice's room. Beatrice's hand slowly made its way towards one of the little drawers in her vanity table.

'Don't,' said Mandrake. I've had enough women drawing blades on me for one day already.'

Beatrice paused and then turned around.

'It's good to see you,' she said. 'It's been quite a while.'

'And you, Beatrice,' Mandrake replied. 'However, I can't stay long. I have quite a few people after me.'

'What do you want?'

'You know me well, Beatrice. It's time for me to disappear for a while. But I've nothing but the clothes I'm wearing and I doubt I'll get much for them. However, the Petraya fortune is close at hand is it not? I'll take your jewels, and any money you have here.'

'Mandrake, is that what you've become? A common thief?'

'Needs must, Bea. Call it payment for your replacement for Aliester.'

She spun round and looked Mandrake in the eye. 'How *dare* you! Aliester is my light and joy!'

'Oh, come now, he's revolting. We both know that. You only keep him alive to scare your servants.'

'How *dare* you Mandrake. Yes, the child is important to

our family, but my Aliester can never be replaced.'

'If you say so, Beatrice. I don't care right now. Your jewels and your money if you please.'

Beatrice Grilsgarter opened a drawer in her vanity table, took out a box, and handed it to Mandrake.

'Here. Take them. Much good they'll do you.'

'Thank you,' said Mandrake turning to leave. 'And I hope the new Aliester is better than the old one.'

'As long as *you* stay away from him he will be,' said Beatrice.

'Oh, that *hurts*, Beatrice, that really does.'

Mandrake left Beatrice Grilsgarter's apartment as quietly as he entered. Beatrice watched him go and smiled.

'Mandrake,' she said to herself. 'Do you know what's wrong with you? You always think everyone else is more stupid than you. I almost feel sorry for you.'

Chapter Twenty-Six: Saviours

'It's a *baby*,' said Ludwig.

Eleni saw Ludwig was right. On the other side of the glass was a young child huddled up inside the egg. Its legs and arms were crossed around itself and its head was tucked in, but it could look up just enough to meet their eyes. Tubes came out of the baby's nose and mouth.

'That's awful!' cried Eleni. 'We have to get it out of there!' Around the egg was a thin join with screws along one side.

Elini darted back to the nearby tables, found a couple of screwdrivers underneath a pile of clutter and came back. She passed one to Ludwig and they both took a side each, quickly twisting their screwdrivers and getting the screws out as fast as they could.

'Be careful,' said Ludwig, eyeing the tubes suspiciously.

'I know!' said Eleni.

Soon enough, all the screws were out. Ludwig and Eleni jumped as the machines around the egg started making more noise. Inside the egg, the liquid that surrounded the baby drained away and the tubes slid out of its mouth and nose.

The egg cracked open and a wail echoed through the villa.

As Mandrake crept through the dark corridors, he heard the baby's cry.

'What have you done!' came Beatrice's voice from a few rooms away. 'It's too soon!'

Mandrake ignored her. The Grilsgarters were not his problem any more. He looked down at the jewellery case and smiled to himself. The Petraya jewels were worth millions. He could hide in the far corners of the earth with this fortune.

'Perhaps things have turned out for the best after all,' said Mandrake to himself. He opened the jewellery case. There was a click and a hiss.

Ludwig scooped up the baby and wrapped it in his jacket.

'What were they doing to him?' asked Eleni, peering down at the young child.

'I don't know,' said Ludwig. 'But we can't leave him here.'

Eleni nodded.

'No. Come on, we've still got to find everyone.'

They found themselves in the corridor once again. At the other end, a couple of Grilsgarter's men rounded the corner.

'Hey!' one of them called out.

Eleni ran at them. After a few swishes of her sword, they fell to the floor in a heap. One of the men groaned. Eleni reached down and pulled him up.

'Where's Grilsgarter?' she shouted into his face.

The man's face was white from the deep cut in his shoulder. He looked up, saw the terrible girl, then he whimpered and tried to crawl away. Eleni shook him.

'Where is he? I'll skin you alive if you don't—'

'Through there!' shouted the man, pointed a shaking finger to an archway some distance away.

'And your prisoners?'

'Down below. The dungeons.'

'Good.'

Eleni turned to Ludwig. 'You still have your pistol?'

Ludwig nodded. Eleni pointed at a nearby stairwell.

'Go down and find my dad. Grilsgarter is mine,' snapped Eleni. 'Then we'll get your dad. He can't have gone far.'

Ludwig headed to the stairwell Eleni's victim had pointed at and went down. Right now, he didn't know who he was more afraid of, Grilsgarter or the Captain's daughter.

Meanwhile, Eleni went to the arch and slipped through; her sabre held firmly in her hand. She gave herself a grim smile as she thought of the terrible things she would do to this Grilsgarter, the pain she would inflict for what he did to her mother and for destroying her life.

On the other side of the arch she was surprised to find herself in a great glass room full of plants and flowers; broad leaves and bright petals hung all around. There were even trees here, reaching up to a ceiling so high even the uppermost leaves didn't touch it. The ceiling itself was a lattice-work of iron beams holding the glass in place that looked like an eight-pointed star stretching up to the roof's pinnacle. On the end of each point of the star, iron pillars ran down until they disappeared behind the foliage.

In front of her, the plants had been cut back and a path snaked deeper into the room. Should she take it, she wondered. If she did, she might bump into someone she'd rather not; any element of surprise gone. Instead, she looked at the undergrowth, gritted her teeth and dived in.

At the bottom of the stairs, Ludwig came to a cavernous room where, shackled to the floor, he found his brother and Sir Notsworth. He saw the Captain pinned to the back wall.

'Ludwig!' the Captain cried out.

'Ludwig?' said Sir Notsworth, looking round. 'Ludwig, my boy!'

Ludwig ran to the desk in the corner of the room and found a set of keys. He grabbed them and unlocked Sir Notsworth's shackles. Then he went over to Hephaestus. Ludwig's brother was huddled up as the baby had been, his legs curled up to his body and his arms wrapped around them. His head was tucked in. Ludwig reached out and touched him on the shoulder.

'Hephaestus? It's me,' said Ludwig. 'We're getting out of here!'

'Hang on, lad,' said Sir Notsworth. He went over to Hephaestus, leant down, and whispered something in his ear. Hephaestus stirred and looked up.

'Ludwig?' he said through tear-stained eyes. 'Ludwig! You're here!'

Ludwig unlocked Hephaestus' shackles and let him get up.

Once Hephaestus was standing, Ludwig hugged him with one hand while holding the baby in the other.

'What have you got there?' asked Hephaestus, peering into the bundle in Ludwig's arms.

'I– I found him,' said Ludwig.

Hephaestus looked horrified. 'Where, Ludwig?'

Ludwig told them about the egg and what he and Eleni had done.

'We should leave it here,' said Hephaestus sadly. 'This is where is belongs.'

'No!' said Ludwig, holding the baby close to him. 'We can't!'

'Ludwig-' began Hephaestus. Ludwig could see the tears in his brother's eyes.

'Easy, Hephaestus,' said Sir Notsworth.

Hephaestus looked at Sir Notsworth then at Ludwig and the child.

'You know what it is.'

'It's just a baby, Hephaestus,' said Sir Notsworth. 'That's all.'

Hephaestus looked at the baby again and then at Ludwig. 'You'd better look after him.'

Ludwig nodded.

'Excuse me, mates,' said the Captain, all but forgotten on the other side of the room.

Ludwig ran over and unlocked the bars that had held the Captain in place.

'Ah!' said the Captain. 'That's better. Now yer'd better tell us what's goin' on?'

Ludwig told them everything, from the crewman returning to his father's escape, and finding the baby in the laboratory.

'Eleni's here?' said the Captain. 'Where is she?'

Ludwig looked up. 'She's gone after Grilsgarter,' he said

'He'll kill her!' shouted the Captain. He turned and bolted up the stairs. The others followed.

Chapter Twenty-Seven:
The End of a Dynasty

Beatrice Grilsgarter ran from her room towards the laboratory. As she ran there was thump nearby. She guessed what must have made the noise but ignored it. There were more important things to deal with.

When she got to the laboratory, she saw the metal egg split open and its liquids spread across the floor. She dropped to the ground and started scrabbling about.

'Where is he?!' she mumbled to herself, pulling her fingers through her hair. 'Where is he? Mandrake, death is too good for you! You've brought ruin again!'

All those years of waiting for Mandrake to succeed, she thought to herself. All that time worrying and fretting whether the Petraya line would continue or be buried once and for all. Mandrake had taken her good sweet child; or he might as well have done, placing Aliester in harm's way.

But afterwards, he had offered hope. It had kept her alive. Mandrake created Hephaestus. He created a child from the remains of his own father. If he could do that then the family could survive. But then Hephaestus had changed and she had despaired.

And then there was Ludwig.

Mandrake had tried again. To create a normal child this time, not perfection as he had done with Hephaestus and failed. That was enough. She didn't need perfection. And... and the next thing she knew Mandrake had forgotten her! He had left her to rot out here in the middle of nowhere while he tried to take over the world with his...his toys, while she hid from those who still wanted her family dead with only a few faithful servants and a corrupted son for company. Mandrake had taken her beloved Aliester and replaced him with... with a machine!

She felt ill whenever she thought of him. She knew Aliester was still there, haunting that mechanical skeleton, but every time she saw his corpse hanging from it like some grotesque ornament it reminded her Aliester was all but gone.

There was a roar and goosebumps rose on her arms and neck.

'Aliester...!'

Eleni slid through the undergrowth of the glasshouse on her stomach. She was filthy, but she didn't care. All that mattered was getting to Grilsgarter.

Eventually, the plants thinned out. She stayed low and peered out from under a large leaf. Beyond was a large clearing with butterflies fluttering to and fro, gliding from flower to flower then to tables where fruit had been left out to attract them.

And there was Aliester Grilsgarter. He was sitting in the middle of the clearing with his back to Eleni and with his legs splayed out in front of him.

Then Eleni noticed something quite strange. Aliester was making no noise and he was very still. The butterflies were happy to land on him and not leave for quite some time. Eleni had been told about the machine, but she wasn't prepared for the nightmare creature ahead of her.

Eleni quietly stood up, drew her sabre and tip-toed closer. She dared not breathe in case the monstrous machine heard her. Soon enough she was standing right behind Grilsgarter. He was hers! She pulled her back her arm. This was it. The creature that had taken her mother from her would perish. Once he was gone, she would find her dad and... and then what? She paused. What would happen next? Would she go back to Guly Porta? She wasn't sure, after what she'd seen in her mother's house. Her gang could look after themselves, but what about Desses? And what about dad? He had reappeared again and even if he was encased in a strange mechanical body, it was still him. She breathed in. The future would have to wait.

She looked at Grilsgarter's back and suddenly a thought occurred to her.

Where should she strike? Grilsgarter's back was a mass of metal, tubes and wires. What would kill him? She wondered. She had no idea.

She closed her eyes, brought up her blade and slashed down, hoping she would damage Aliester enough to finish him off. Eleni jumped back as Aliester woke and roared out in surprise. Wires pinged and tubes spewed out vile-smelling liquid.

'Get away from me!' Aliester screeched, turning towards her.

'This is for my mother!' screamed Eleni. Aliester lashed out and Eleni jumped out of the way as one of his huge fists came crashing down, burying itself in the grass.

'Your mother?' said Grilsgarter, swiping at Eleni again and smashing into a nearby tree. The tree tumbled down and the butterflies scattered.

'Rosiet!' Eleni shouted, swinging her blade time and time again at Aliester's piston arms. She was furious now, spinning, weaving and diving. Aliester couldn't get near her.

'Stay still!' he whined.

Eleni dodged left and Aliester's fists crashed down again. But she was too slow for the other. It slammed into her, pinning her to the ground.

Grilsgarter lent over her, his body spluttering and bleeding a flow of black liquid over the ground.

'I'm going to *enjoy* this,' spluttered Aliester. His hand shot out at lightening speed. Eleni's sabre buried itself into Aliester's arm but not before he'd knocked her down again.

'I'm going to tear you apart like an insect. I shouldn't have let Ekhert finish your mother off. He did it quick; peaceful. I should have made her scream!'

Eleni, terrified now, tugged at her sabre but it wouldn't come loose as the brutal pressure of Grilsgarter held her down.

Eleni twisted her head and so did Aliester. There was her father - the Captain - running straight at them. He crashed into Grilsgarter and Eleni dived out of the way, her legs now free from the creature's grasp. She watched as Grilsgarter and her father rolled away, both striking each other with all their might.

'How dare yer touch her!' cried the Captain, pushing Aliester back.

Aliester tore into the Captain smashing him to the ground. 'That body of yours doesn't seem quite as good as I would have thought,' screeched Aliester.

The Captain fell back. Aliester was right. The Captain couldn't fight him. Grilsgarter was massive and powerful, even when wounded. The Captain turned to her.

'Go! Get back to the *Kamaria*!'

'No!' shouted Eleni. 'He's already had one of my parents!' She drove forward.

While Grilsgarter was busy with her father, Eleni circled around trying to find some weakness in the creatures' lumbering body. Aliester saw her and moved, making sure both father and daughter were in his sight.

'You will suffer for this intrusion!' Grilsgarter screamed at them.

Ludwig stood watching the battle between Eleni, the Captain and Grilsgarter. The ferocity of it shocked him.

In his hands, the baby squirmed.

'Don't worry,' said Ludwig. 'The Captain and Eleni will win, you'll see. They have to.'

There was a noise beside him. Ludwig turned and saw a woman appear on the path leading back into the villa. His eyes met the woman's, then her mouth gaped open. She pointed at the bundle in his hands.

'The child,' she shouted. 'Give me back my child!'

Ludwig and Beatrice watched stunned as Aliester stopped struggling. Even the baby in his arms stopped squirming, as if it knew something momentous had just happened.

'Aliester!' the woman next to Ludwig cried. She ran past him towards the fallen creature. 'Oh, Aliester,' she whimpered, dropping to her knees. She reached out and stroked Aliester's head. 'Don't leave me my sweetness.'

The Captain and Eleni got up and left the grieving woman in peace. They came up to the others.

'It's over,' said the Captain. He looked back at Aliester and his mother, then at the baby in Ludwig's arms. 'I don't know how I'm goin' to explain all this back home.'

'We've still got one more thing to do,' said Hephaestus.

'I know, mate,' replied the Captain. 'I hadn't forgotten. Mandrake.'

'Where do you think he is?' asked Sir Notsworth.

'I've no idea,' said the Captain. 'For all we know he's left the villa already.'

'So we've lost him again,' replied Hephaestus angrily. 'I'm tired of chasing him!'

Suddenly a thought came to Ludwig. He reached into his pocket and pulled out the little HELOT.

'Wait!' he called out. 'I've got an idea!'

'What have yer got there?' said the Captain.

Hephaestus looked in Ludwig's hand and his eyes widened. 'Ludwig! You found the prototype! When?'

Ludwig told them about finding the little HELOT in their old home.

'You...you have to destroy it,' said Hephaestus quietly. 'Do you know what would happen if someone got hold of that?' Ludwig nodded.

'I know, but I couldn't bring myself to get rid of it. I'm glad I didn't. Watch; it could help us.'

He placed the little HELOT on the ground and it scurried off back into the villa.

'Follow it!' said Ludwig.

'What are you up to, mate?' said the Captain as they chased the little HELOT.

'Trust me,' said Ludwig. They followed the little HELOT up flights of stairs and down corridors. Soon enough, the HELOT disappeared into one room.

'He's in there, I'm sure of it,' whispered Ludwig.

'Wait here,' said the Captain. 'He might be armed.'

The Captain and Sir Notsworth disappeared into the room. Ludwig had braced himself for a fight, instead he heard:

'Ludwig, Hephaestus, you'd better come here,' came the Captain's voice.

Ludwig felt a lump in his throat. He recognised that tone. He'd heard it a week or so ago.

He went forward into the room. At the far end he saw the little HELOT nudging up against his father. His father was lying still on the floor. By his side was a jewellery box half-open. Sticking out of it was a long thin blade.

'Is he...?' began Ludwig,

The Captain nodded.

'Yes, mate. I'm sorry.' He picked up the jewellery box. 'This was booby-trapped.'

'I can't believe it,' whispered Ludwig. 'He's dead.'

'Good,' said Hephaestus, coming up behind Ludwig. 'Don't look at me like that. It had to happen sooner or later. 'I hated him, Ludwig; more than you could possibly know.'

The Captain reached out and picked up Mandrake's body.

'We should take him back,' he said. 'Your grandmother will want to say goodbye to him. Let's go home.'

Epilogue:

Hephaestus sat in his cabin in darkness. He had been silent as they had travelled back to the *Kamaria*, and when they were aboard, he had left everyone else straight away.

What am I? He thought. *I'm not a person. I'm just a copy; a mistake...*

The enormity of what he had learned felt like a lead weight around his neck, drowning him.

Ludwig must never know.

He was brought to his senses by a knock at the door.

'Go away,' he called out, but no one replied. Instead there was a shuffling sound and a note appeared at the foot of his cabin door.

Hephaestus picked up the note then opened the door. There was no one in the corridor outside. After closing the door again, he opened the note.

Dear Hephaestus

I have come to learn that you were responsible for the creation of the HELOTs. As you can surely appreciate, I doubt you would like this knowledge to become public; therefore I have a proposal for you . . .

Also by this author:

HAYWIRED
By Alex Keller

In the quiet village of Little Wainesford, Ludwig von Guggenstein is about to have his unusual existence turned inside out. When he and his father are blamed for a fatal accident during the harvest, a monstrous family secret is revealed. Soon Ludwig will begin to uncover diabolical plans that span countries and generations while ghoulish machines hunt him down. He must fight for survival, in a world gone haywire.

ISBN: 978-1-906132-33-0
UK: £7.99

http://www.mogzilla.co.uk/haywired

Also from Mogzilla:

By Robin Price & Paul McGrory

Jemima Mallard is having a bad day. First she loses her air, then someone steals her houseboat, and now the Youth Cops think she's mixed up with a criminal called Father Thames. Not even her dad, a Chief Inspector with the 'Dult Police, can help her out this time. Oh – and London's still sinking. It's been underwater ever since the climate upgrade. All in all, it's looking like deep trouble.

ISBN: 978-1-906132-03-3

Chosen as a 'Recommended Read' for World Book Day 2011. One of the *Manchester Book Award's* 24 recommended titles for. 2010.

'This is a terrifically atmospheric page-turning adventure told with words and comic art... it's a rattling good read and one in which you are sure to be drawn into Jemima's exploits of survival.' – *Lovereading.co.uk*

BOUDICAT

Rome AD 36. The mighty Feline Empire rules the world. Queen Boudicat has declared war on Rome and wants Spartapuss to join her rebel army. Our ginger hero can't see how a tiny tribe of Kitons can take on the mighty Feline Empire. But warrior queens don't take 'No' for an answer. Boudicat is not for turning, she's for burning! Action-packed and full of historical details, the Spartapuss series follows the diary of a gladiator cat from Rome to the Land of the Kitons (A.K.A. Britain). Boudicat, the fourth book in the Spartapuss series, was awarded an 'Exclusively Independent' pick of the month for July 2009.

"An exciting series... really good books. I would recommend them to 10 year olds and upwards who enjoy thrillers that you can't put down 'til you've read the whole thing!" – Flora Murray, Dalry Secondary School S1, *The Journal of Classics Teaching*

ISBN: 9781906132019
UK £6.99
USA $14.95/ CAN $16.95

DIE CLAWDIUS

In the third installment of the series, six-clawed hero
Spartapuss is horrified to find that the Emperor is planning
an invasion of the Land of the Kitons, aka Great Britain.
Clawdius, the least likely emperor in Roman history, needs
to show his enemies who is boss. While Spartapuss has
always wanted to visit his birthplace--famous for its terrible
food, evil weather, and the tuneless howling of its savage
tribes--he is loath to journey there as part of an invasion.
However, he soon finds himself rounded up and forced
aboard the first ship in the invasion fleet and part of the
landing party that sets out to search for the Kiton Army.
Soon captured by two warriors, Spartapuss escapes into
the woods, where he meets Furg, a young Kiton study-
ing to become a Mewid. After joining a Mewid school,
Spartapuss realises he must choose between his new
friends and the Emperor. Can the magic of the Mewids
help him make the right decision?

'Another fantastic story in this brilliantly inventive
series!' - *Teaching and Learning Magazine*

ISBN: 9780954657680
UK £6.99
USA $14.95/ CAN $16.95

CATLIGULA

In the second book in the Spartapuss series, history takes a terrible turn for the worse as Catligula becomes Emperor. Rome's new ruler is mad, bad and dangerous to stroke. When Spartapuss starts a new job at the Imperial Palace, he is horrified to find that Catligula wants him as his new best friend. The Spraetorian Guard plot to tame the power-crazed puss before he ruins the Empire. But will Spartapuss play ball?

'Cat-tastic!' - *London Evening Standard*

ISBN: 9780954657611
UK £7.99
USA: $14.95/ CAN $16.95

I AM SPARTAPUSS

In the first adventure in the Spartapuss series...
Rome AD 36. The mighty Feline Empire rules the world.
Spartapuss, a ginger cat is comfortable managing Rome's
finest Bath and Spa. But Fortune has other plans for him.
Spartapuss is arrested and imprisoned by Catligula, the
Emperor's heir. Sent to a school for gladiators, he must fight
and win his freedom in the Arena - before his opponents
make dog food out of him.

'This witty Roman romp is history with cattitude.'
Junior Magazine (Scholastic)

ISBN: 978-0-9546576-0-4
UK: £7.99
USA: $14.95/ CAN $16.95

In Volume II of 'London Deep'...

FATHER THAMES

Rebellious teen Jemima Mallard has done the unthinkable. She's joined the Youth Police Department (YPD).

Is she serious, or is she spying for the criminal Father Thames? Fellow YPD officer Nick Mallard isn't sure. Before he can test her loyalty, the two must go to war.

Their city is under attack. From the Thames Barrier Reef to the Sink estates, strange ships have breached the defences. London hasn't seen anything like these raiders – adults and kids sailing and working together. But orders are orders, Jem must find find a way to stop them.

ISBN: 978-1-906132-04-0
Price: £7.99

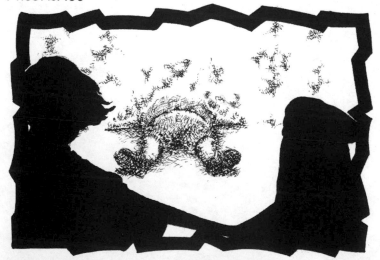